e.a.r.t.h.

by
arthur douglas

*for all those
who have spent more than 14.67 seconds
contemplating the meaning of life*

Order this book online at www.trafford.com
or email orders@trafford.com

Most Trafford titles are also available at major online book retailers.

Printed in the United States of America.

ISBN: 978-1-4251-9139-9 (sc)
ISBN: 978-1-4269-1118-7 (e)

Trafford rev. 04/11/2014

 www.trafford.com

North America & international
toll-free: 1 888 232 4444 (USA & Canada)
fax: 812 355 4082

introduction

when quark asked me to write an introduction for this story i had no idea what to say ... or if anything i could say would be useful ... further to that i questioned my qualifications to speak about earth at all ... but then i reasoned that sometimes we leave things unsaid that should be said ... so surely i could find a few words even in this strange tongue to honor a bargain struck with one of your kind ... aGnos ... like earth is a blue planet ... it is a delicate mix of harsh and serene ... it is at first glance an endless vista of sustenance for its homo sapiens populations to enjoy ... in fact ... there was a time ... long ago on aGnos when it was believed that her heart and wealth was infinite ... and worse her populations found excuses to fight over that perceived wealth ... it would be nice to record that there was some single event that changed all this ... but there was not ... what there was ... was the slow realization that to survive every one had to get onto the same page ... it was not a matter of a poorer part trading with a richer part ... because one way or another everything ... made ... traded or sold really came from the living planet ... if the planet became ill from the activities of its animal populations those populations suffer as well ... and aGnos was most assuredly ill ... her populations ... if not physically ill ... were ill in spirit ... homo sapiens are at best triumphs of adaptive evolution ... at worst they are ungiving possessive animals with a chemical driven need to perpetuate their kind ... this is not all bad ... but it presents a dilemma for judgment ... how far in any one direction is too far ... slowly the populations of

2

aGnos began to see that they all needed a fair cut of the planetary cake ... and for the sake of that cake ... they would need to take care of its source ... aGnos itself ... if this was to happen they would have to set aside the engines of personal and national division and work together ... slowly they began to undivide themselves and think of themselves as aGnosics first and their region of origin second ... they came to see that their domestic arguments were trivial compared with their mutual need of cooperation to save their planet for their own survival ... these old dark days of aGnos ... still shape our thinking ... we steer away from all forms of dogma ... there are no symbols of status in our language ... all our people are equal before a global law ... we encourage all forms of endeavour that free us to live on the planet and not from the planet ... we care for our planet as a living being ... these are some of our solutions ... but the universe is vast there are many others ... what works for us may not work for others ... but one thing is clear the underlying engine of peace is the individual.

eva lution   aGnos

realtime aGnos

>fellow beings and entities ... as the current coordinator of the b.I.d ... it fell to me to carry out the council's wishes regarding the experiment to alleviate racial tension and hatred ... and as far as i know ... none of us need reminding how close we are to the end of our deal with the ... fractious four ... you will recall ... at a previous meeting we selected quark quasar to obtain the latest data on the experiment ... and for security reasons filed his report to my memcode[1] only ... his initial data was useless ... i reminded him how volatile our circumstances could become if the fractious four got the idea that the e.a.r.t.h. was unlikely to have a positive outcome ... i suggested he should get closer ... more personal ... to see if e.a.r.t.h.lings ... i suppose by now we should feel them to be earthlings...could truly communicate or network ... and before you remind me ... i know ... getting so close was the way we lost crystal ... i suggested that he may be able to join with a domestic dog ... via a membrain link ... his first attempts were with homeless dogs and far less than successful ... he suffered various degrees of fear ... hunger ... rejection and abuse that left him close to despair then ... he met a dog called Mac ... Mac and a female earthling had encountered the corpse of the dog who had been quark's last host ... quark immediately detected intense sorrow and sympathy from both Mac and the girl ... for the next few days

---

[1] *memcode: a digitized spectroscopy of amplified brain patterns as hosted by a carrier frequency analogous to the color spectrum but slightly red shifted.*

quark observed them with caution ... he began to feel that whatever it was between the dog and the girl transcended anything he had seen so far ... indeed ... it may have been a true example of networking ... he began to feel that he was prying into something too private to notice ... quark spent much of that week in indecision ... on the one hand he needed to find something positive ... and on the other he didn't want to touch this relationship ... it seemed to contain what he was looking for and he was afraid to find it an illusion ... events ... as they do ... finally made the decision for him ... walking home one evening the girl was attacked by two angry looking youths ... thugs trying to steal her wallet ... Mac threw himself forward ... gripping the forearm of one ... while the other moved quickly toward Kate... the incident was brief but telling ... so at this point i will turn the story over to membrain who has placed the whole file into memrec ... this way you will travel with and experience the events as they subsequently happened ... for reasons of logic and security the voices will remain in their native tongue ... and other reasons that will become clear ... membrain has tagged and coded each speaker so that they are more clearly defined ... for here and earth ... we have done similar with past situations ... but none as potentially difficult as this ... it is hoped that this virtual communication will suffice to protect our meeting from mergoplan ... probes long enough for us to conclude a plan of action ... the data stream starts with the first meeting between quark and the earth dog ... Mac <

memtime ... sector one ... level one ... code two.

quark	*>need some help<*
Mac	Stupid bloody question. Why don't you take care of the other one?
quark	*>i've just asked membrain to edit the other's thinking for him<*
memnote	*>suddenly ... both youths turned and fled ... leaving the girl shaken but unharmed<* end *memnote*
Mac	Whew. Thanks .. I think. You've been hovering about for a week, haven't you? I figured you had to say hello sooner or later. Who the hell are you anyway?
quark	*>i'm quark quasar from the planet aGnos<*
Mac	Agnos, ah. i spoke to a guy from Splagvoid once. He was here doing an environmental study. Seems they were thinking of upgrading mars to habitable. He was a good bloke. Do you know that planet?
quark	*>yes ... and they decided not to go ahead when they figured out who their neighbours would be<*
Mac	makes sense. Are you coming home with us or what?
quark	*>i would like to talk with you later<*
Mac	As long as you don't mind dog food.
quark	*>well ... i'm with you ... but not of you so it won't worry me<*

memnote >*Mac's openness suggested that just maybe the experiment to alleviate racial tension and hatred still had a chance ... unbeknown to the girl i went with them ... they had a small flat in an old building near the city centre ... by the time they got home it was clear that the attack had shaken her ... she sank to the carpet ... holding Mac tight*< end memnote

Kate Oh Mac, why do sighted people waste so much on anger? All some of them see when they look around is something to steal or break. There's so much beauty around them they can't see it. Sometimes i think that only blind people can really see. People should try at least one day of their lives in a blindfold to remind them what having sight really means. if someone offered me sight for the rest of my life i would trade it all for just one day if that meant everyone else could have one day of blindness.

memnote >*she cried ... and then fell silent ... after a while the phone rang ... earthlings have not developed memory or thought transmission ... so they use of a device they call a telephone ... the caller was her mother ... and as i was to find out ... she was sounding an old tone*< end memnote

Mum i just don't know why you want to live in the city, dear. it's so difficult even for sighted people and you know how dangerous the streets can be at night. If

	something were to happen, Mac could not protect you. You should come home, dear.
Kate	Oh, Mum. We've done all this before. You know I hate to feel dependent on anyone, and we don't get along – we never have. What makes you think it would be any better if I came home now?
quark	>what's her mother like<
Mac	She's one of those people who could dramatize buying a flea collar.

memnote	>i realized that the girl ... who had gone through a considerable scare only a short time before ... still preferred her way of life with her guide dog to the security of her mother's home ... there was something there that i had not noticed before ... she finished the phone conversation and turned to Mac< end memnote

Kate	You know, Mac, if we went home it would be fine for a week and then Mum would start telling me that you smell and that I should give up and get married. Oh, Mac ... I can't spend the rest of my life wondering whether a man married me for love or pity when I don't pity myself. That's Mother's trip, not mine. Come on Mac, let's get your dinner now.

memnote	>i tried to imagine what it would be like to be unable to see ... it crossed my senses that here was a person striving to lead a normal life and in that effort she was achieving something far greater than

anything i had seen so far ...it made me feel sad for those young thugs who attacked her ... sad, because they were handicapped much more than she was ...apparently they lacked the ability or the imagination to be any more than cowards and thieves ...i began to see Kate as an alien ... like me ... a being trying to come to terms with a confusing world ... but unlike the thugs she had not given up ...she responded with courage and peace ... not fear and anger ...i knew i needed to know more about her< end memnote

quark   *>Mac ... what's her father like<*
Mac   He died before I came on duty but according to his Labrador he was a very peaceful fellow, not given to flights of fancy. He had great emotional depth.
          Do you understand emotional? I know not all aliens do.
quark   *>i know what you mean<*

memnote   *>the next morning i went with Kate and Mac the few blocks to her work ... they stopped at the spot where the attack had occurred<* end memnote

Kate   What happened to the other one, Mac? Why didn't he take his chance with me when you had his mate bailed up? I wonder if I should report it to the police ...
          ...

memnote   *>she hesitated ... thoughtfully fondling Mac's head ...there it was again ... the*

9

willingness to understand rather than just react< end *memnote*

Kate   ... mmmm, no ... I suppose it would only be more information for mother. Grist for her mill. We'd be fighting all over again. Life's too short to be fighting with her over whether or not I have a right to a life of my own.

memnote *>she drew herself up and lifted her head towards the sky ... giving herself a little shake at the shoulder ... Mac responded instinctively<* end *memnote*

Kate   No Mac ... I think we'll just let it go.
Come on, we'll be late. This job was too long in the making to lose it now.

Mac   Are you going to tell her what happened?

quark *>yes ... but not yet<*

Mac   You did help save her last night so I guess I can trust you.

memnote *>Kate worked as a receptionist in a small office ... meeting visitors and operating the phone system ... as soon as she arrived that morning her supervisor asked her to see him in his office<* end *memnote*

quark *>Mac ... go with her so i can feel what's happening<*

Mr. J   Kate, I've had the police here this morning telling me that you had an incident with a couple of muggers last night. it was reported to the police by someone driving past but before he could stop to help Mac had driven them off and he wasn't sure he should approach you. He thought he might frighten you further so he followed until you entered your building. Then he called the police.

Kate   That's true, but why would the police talk to you about it<

Mr. J   I gather their informant works or lives around here and knows that you work here. Given the crime rate he felt strongly enough to report what he saw. You're an easy target, Kate. Too easy.

Kate   Mr. James, what's the problem? Are you worried because I was attacked? I wasn't hurt. I'm probably safer than a sighted person because of Mac. I'd be more worried if I was sighted. I'm twenty nine and I've been taking care of myself for a long time. What happened last night could happen to anyone, anywhere.

memnote   >*again ... there it was ... something about her*< end memnote

Kate   I'm touched by your concern, Mr. James, but it's not going to protect me ... please, what are you meaning to say?

Mr. J   Kate, the company feels that it can't ask you to put yourself at risk any more...

Kate   ...are you sacking me because I'm blind and you think I'm a target for street attackers? I've been walking here with Mac for years, dodging trucks and buses. You know that. Was the possibility of being run over far

	less horrible than the idea that I might be mugged in public and drag the company name into the press?
Mr. J	I am sorry, Kate, but the company has a duty of care to all employees. If it was up to me I would keep you on but the decision is out of my hands.
Kate	Mr. James, I was born blind, not stupid. My father used to say that no one could blame me if I wanted to take life easy. He supported every decision I made and he helped me realize that one way or another all of mankind is blind.
memnote	>the supervisor had the grace to look ashamed ... he stood up with his hands extended in a pleading gesture ... i saw that he was unnerved by Kate's sightless eyes fixed at a point above his sweating brow< end memnote
Kate	Mankind is blind. My only difficulty has been what I made of it. My future is in my hands. Determination to do something with my life would have to come from me – no one was going to put it there. I could have quit long ago but I didn't. So it really burns my butt when someone quits for me..
Mr. J	Kate, I'll talk to them, see if I can get them to change their minds.
Kate	Please don't bother now Mr. James. Your company doesn't deserve me. I'm resigning, as of now..
memnote	>as if they were one being Kate and Mac spun about and walked out ... passing the

manager's office ... stopping only long
enough for Kate's desk to retrieve a couple
of personal items< end memnote

Mac   Sacked for being blind.
quark   *>this planet never fails to disappoint me<*
Mac   Don't be too hard on them.   They're only
           human after all.

memnote   *>back out in the street Kate chattered*
           nervously, saying she was sure no one
           wanted to be blind ... there was no point
           being angry over something you couldn't
           change ...that was wasted energy and
           frustration ... the most frustrating thing by
           far was to put up with the James' of this
           world< end memnote

Kate   In fact, he and Mother would make a good
           pair.   They could spend their lives being
           frightened of each other's shadows.   Well
           Mac, you're OK for a while.   There's plenty
           of food for you in the cupboard and if worse
           comes to worst we can sell the silver and
           the Ming vase and go home to Mother,
           perish the thought.   Oh well, that's
           Monday's dilemma.
Mac   I'm thinking, do you do tricks?   Because if I
           know my girl, she'll go home, put it all out
           of her mind and come Monday start looking
           for another job, and only when she finds
           one will she tell anyone what happened.
           Sometimes she's just too tough for her own
           good.
quark   *>what do you want me to do<*

Mac	The only person she would tell is her sister Ann; she's an artist, they go to the Art gallery sometimes. Kate likes her sister's descriptions of other artist's monstrosities, as Ann sometimes calls them. Kate says Ann might be jealous because her stuff does not get into the gallery, but it cheers her up and she always enjoys it. She won't call Ann first and Ann won't call her at home in the middle of a work day for obvious reasons.
quark	*>what would a blind person want in an art gallery<*
Mac	She says to feel close to aspirations although some of the stuff I wouldn't bring to a dog's dunny. Anyway you haven't answered my question.
quark	*>you want me to get her to call her sister ... right ... i can't do that without giving myself away<*
Mac	Can't a smart alien like you figure something out?

memnote	*>Mac's concern for Kate was appealing and refreshing ... i had to do what i could ... when they got home ... Mac made a beeline for his food bowl, making more fuss about it than usual ... his behavior distracted her<* *end memnote*

Kate	Mac, this is no time for you to start associating unemployment with long lunches. Okay, okay, I'm getting it.
Mac	Okay, okay, now's our chance.
quark	*>chance for what ... Mac<*

14

Mac	For the brilliant plan you've come up with? What are we going to do<
quark	>can you use the phone<
Mac	Sure. Ann's number is the first key. I can get the handset off ... but this is a very low-tech plan. Then what?
quark	>but it's simple and straight forward ... if you want to call get moving<
Mac	It's ringing...now what?
Ann	Hello, hello ... HELLO?? Who is this? Oh for heaven's sake go breathe somewhere else.
Kate	Mac, what was that? Are you playing with the phone again? You are funny ...
Mac	That was close. What did you do<
quark	>i had a friend make a suggestion ... just wait ... Ann's about to call<
Mac	I hope so.
memnote	>Kate was placing Mac's bowl down when the phone jangled< end memnote
Kate	Here Mac ... oh, not again ... hellooo ?... Oh, hi Ann. How did you know I was home?
Ann	I didn't .. I had another sudden impulse ... I 'm getting them more than ever since Tony went back to his mousy wife ... but how are you, and why are you at home to answer the phone?
Kate	Apart from being sacked, I'm fine ... well I was going to be sacked. so I quit.
Ann	No. I don't believe it. What for? Have you told mother?
Kate	No, I haven't told mother, and I'm not going to if I can help it. I'll have to find another

15

job quick smart but why don't we celebrate our mutual new found freedom tomorrow? Let's go to lunch and the art gallery afterwards.

Ann   Okay, but let's have lunch here first so we can talk for a while and I'll show you my latest creation. I can't wait to hear what happened with old James. Oh, you poor thing.

Kate   What time do you get out of bed these days? I would hate to get you up too early; you might stay grumpy all day.

Ann   Why don't you come over around ten? That should give us plenty of time to talk, get lunch and go out later, if we still want to. Take care now, and give Mac a hug for me. See you later.

quark   *>i told you it would work<*

Mac   I suppose, but I think it owes more to cheek than class.

memnote   *>the next day it began to rain heavily ... so ... Kate and Mac took a taxi to Ann's studio ... Kate told Ann how she had been attacked and how Mac had defended her ... she said how strange it was that the other man ran off without taking his chance with her ... while Mac was working on his mate ... she said that it felt eerie ... as if someone else was there as well ... her sister's obvious suggestion was that maybe someone else did come along at that time ... the man in the car could have helped scare them off ... Kate argued that he still had time to grab her wallet before he left ... i was interested to note that Kate suspected that someone*

had helped Mac defend her ... later ... they
discussed Kate's dismissal at work< end
memnote

Ann

Sis, I think you should go to the Equal
Opportunities Board. You've been treated
badly just because you're blind. I'm quite
sure you would win and get your job back.
Despite what old James says, you have
been discriminated against, and you do
have the right to get even.

quark

>Mac ... what's the equal opportunities
board<

Mac

It's a place where humans go to prove that
they're equal.

quark

>pity it's not level<

Kate

I know that, but getting my job back won't
change their minds. It would be like
moving home to mother: she would
welcome me, but not really want me to
stay. Life is too short for all that shit.

Ann

Oh, Kate ... you've always taken life on the
chin. I've always envied that about you, no
matter what life turns your way, you
manage to cope and keep it in
perspective, but, I'll never work out how
you brought yourself to send Ben away. It
seemed to me he was wonderful, all any
woman could want, and he loved you so
much.

quark

>women are the same all over the galaxy<

Mac

Four legged as well.

quark

>not my zone of expertise Mac<

Kate

I know he loved me and never thought of
me as limited or disabled, but there was

	always the fear that one day he would. I loved him too much to let that happen so I gave him back to himself ...
Ann	... but you couldn't know if that would ever happen?
Kate	He would have spent his life serving me, and letting the things he wanted to do go. I will always love him but he is better off in his own world, and I am better off in mine, without the fear that time and familiarity would make our love ordinary. If I ever do marry, it will be to someone who gives me what I need, not what I want.
quark	>your mistress is a romantic<
Mac	I'm only the chauffeur.
Ann	Kate, we all want things; sometimes we need to want things, we can't just live lives of need. It's the little unexpected spicy bits along the way that make life interesting and keep it fresh. Life can't be just one long intellectual parade.
Kate	I'm not saying it should be but to survive we need to exert some degree of logic over ourselves. I want to see, but if I spend all my time wanting what I can't have I'll lose what I need, a productive and rewarding life. Speaking of that, are we going to the gallery, or are we going to bum around here all afternoon?
quark	>she's tough as well<
Mac	Brittle things break.
Ann	I guess if we're going we should get started. it's stopped raining, so we could walk if you like.

18

Kate   Yes let's, everything smells so good after rain, fresh and clean. Besides, Mac has started overeating so a walk will do him good. He may even get a chance to chew on some fresh muggers along the way.

Ann   I wish you wouldn't joke about that. it could have been a lot worse, and next time he may not get help from an unknown source. I don't know how you can treat it so calmly.

Kate   Oh sis, in a city this size we all run the risk of becoming a statistic, that's the way it is. I'm sure it doesn't need to be like that, but some people seem too weak to be honest. it's not so much that people don't care, I think they've just forgotten how, or are afraid to show they do because they might lose face, and that's all some have. Then governments who are supposed to take care take sides, and religion manages to make things worse. I would love to tell those who started that whole concept how wrong they were.

quark   >she's a softie underneath<

Mac   She always gets my dinner first.

memnote   >they walked along ... engrossed in conversation ... stopping here and there to explore some new thing going on in that part of the city ... i was constantly amazed at Kate's breadth of interest ... she would ask how many cranes a building site had ... how deep the excavation was ... how many earthmovers were involved ... her sister never tired of explaining what was going on ... i realized that behind the sightless eyes

19

was a mind with an insatiable thirst for information and experience< end *memnote*

quark   *>Mac ... does she always want to know everything<*

Mac   Only when she's awake.

memnote   *>the gallery was quiet and peaceful ... only subdued murmurings or human comments of surprise or appreciation on the air ... Ann asked Kate what she would like to do first ... but she knew her sister had no preference ... to Kate the gallery was a temple to human aspiration ... for surely no people who honored and protected art could be all bad ... while individuals cared and struggled enough to assemble their thoughts and feelings into some sort of order to produce works of art or conscience ... it seemed to her that the world still had a chance ... i had never thought that way and was curious to know more ... Ann led Kate toward a particular exhibit<* end *memnote*

Ann   Here's something I found last time I came here ...

Kate   What is it<

Ann   It's a statue.   It's a pregnant woman. She's wearing a very ordinary green dress and holding a plastic laundry basket full of washing. There's a box of washing powder beside her.

Kate   You're having me on? What does she look like?

Ann	She looks ... mmm, secondhand and defeated. Her mouth is small and sexless and the horn rimmed glasses are weird, old fashioned. Her hair is in curlers under a red net and a handful of hair has escaped the hair net falling down each pinched cheek to just below her shoulders. The dress is one of those awful dresses they put pregnant women in, as if to say they're on another planet. It always amazes me how women change. She was probably the prettiest woman on the block once; maybe she even had a brain although I doubt she ever got to show it before some male promised her the world and took her away from it at the same time.
quark	>is her sister always so anti-male<
Mac	Only when she's just lost one.
Kate	What's she wearing on her feet?
Ann	Those Dutch clog things with a mesh top.
Kate	Is she short? I feel she's short.
Ann	She's about five feet two without the clogs. Given the chance I'd ban those dresses. I guess it just goes to prove that if God does exist, she is he, because no woman would let her sisters end up like that if she could help it.
Kate	Oh sis, she didn't have to get pregnant, or married. Those decisions were hers to make. Sometimes you're too hard on the world. Besides, so far women are the only ones who can get pregnant, so you can blame biology for that.
Mac	Females have to be more intelligent than males.
quark	>Mac ... why's that<

Mac	To keep them interested in moving targets.
quark	*>well, love is a form of motion sickness Mac<*
Ann	It just annoys me that women are shown as bodies, rather than intelligences. Come on, here's a painting of Hera. According to the ticket, in Greek mythology she was queen of the Gods. The daughter of the Titans Cronus and Rhea, sister and wife of the God Zeus. She was the Goddess of marriage and the protector of married women. Hera was a jealous wife, and often persecuted Zeus' mistresses and children. So what else is new? She was vindictive, and never forgot an injury, and while angry with the Trojan prince Paris for preferring Aphrodite, the Goddess of love to herself, she aided the Greeks in the Trojan War and was not appeased until Troy was finally destroyed. Now that's quite a girl in anyone's century. She could become President of any country; maybe even make her own country first, so why in the late winter of the nineteenth century, did someone paint her as a naked, soft, lily white, out to lunch airhead? I mean, she must have commanded some power; as the story goes she was making it with Zeus. She was the protector of married women, she must have been a strong character. Why show her as insignificant or weak?
quark	*>there is one planet where the population has evolved into hermaphrodites ... and another one where they alternate between male and female<*

22

Mac	That must be confusing.
quark	*>for whom<*
Mac	The carriage trade. Why don't you tell Kate? She will tease her sister with the idea, it should be fun.
quark	*>what if she throws a fit<*
Mac	Not my girl.

memnote	*>at this moment Kate caught herself saying aloud ... Mac, that's the silliest thing you have ever said. ... before she realized it was the only thing he had ever said ... but instinct told her the best way to deal with it then was to say nothing to Ann about how the idea had come to her ... but she teased her sister with it anyway<* end memnote

Kate	Sis, I've just had a funny thought. Imagine if the population alternated between male and female, or even became hermaphrodites, as they supposedly have somewhere in other worlds?
Ann	You haven't been sniffing Mac's flea collar behind my back have you? That's the craziest thing I've ever heard, but it could be a cure for AIDS. It would make virgin birth unremarkable and commonplace. Flipping in and out of gender would bring a whole new meaning to the change of life but what would happen if a boygirl met a girlboy about the time she was going to change into a boygirl herself? You will have to do better than that if you want a government grant to develop that idea. Come on, here's something ...

23

quark	>*you really do know women don't you Mac*<
Mac	I should, I'm a dog, and nothing puts women into perspective more sharply than having to fight for the right.
Kate	Not another lecture on male chauvinism is it, I couldn't cope with another one of those today.
Ann	No it's not, it's a soldier of the First World War. You know, the war to end all wars?
Kate	What's special about him?
Ann	According to the label he was a light horseman, painted by someone who was there at the time.
Kate	Is he young, old, large or small?
Ann	He's not young, but he's not old either. He's sitting down holding a grey felt plumed hat. His sergeant's coat is hanging over the back of the chair; he is wearing a flannel shirt with no collar and he's looking down across his right shoulder. The bottom of the picture does not go much below his right elbow.
Kate	Is he inside or outside?
Ann	He is outside. There is a blue sky with little white clouds. A range of hills comes down on the right-hand side of the picture to behind his left shoulder and then reappears above his right. There is a tumble of rocks on the face of the hill behind his right shoulder. The hills are light brown and in a way he melts into the background, but his head is fully backed by the blue sky.
Kate	He could not be looking down in anger then.

Ann   You're right, there is no anger in his face or
his pose. He's holding his hat with his
right hand, by the top, not the brim, and he
has his left hand on his forearm. His
fingers are long: it's a strong hand. You
can imagine it guiding a plough or swinging
an axe, but it's gentle enough to hold a
child. it's not a self satisfied hand, it's
sensuously strong rather than strongly
sensuous. His head is tilted down as if he
has just caught a glimpse of something.

Kate   Is he lost, or is he lost in thought?

Ann   I don't know that he's either. He is
thinking, but he seems to be looking at a
reminder of something, not of something he
has forgotten, something he is seeing in a
different way. He's not looking down to
look down on some person, he's not looking
out of himself in shame, or anything, at
being   a   soldier,   there   is
completeness in him. He is not in awe of
anything. it's like he was called on to do
something, something much older than he,
something he alone could not change,
something he participates in because a
condition exists. Like when you are ill,
and want to be well, you know it will take
time and impatience will get you nowhere.
Then one day you will be better because
you have a duty to yourself to be well, and
that ultimately makes you well. He is the
same: he sees the sickness, it envelops
him, but does not overcome him. He does
not accept or reject, he is not a crusader or
an avenger, he is not invulnerable, and he
has no look of wanting to be. In many ways

	he is just a peaceful man caught up in a madness and he is resolved to bear it, to apportion no guilt or innocence, but just endure until it is past.
Kate	What do you think he would say if he were to speak?
Ann	I don't know.
Kate	I think he'd say something like, 'Come on boy, let's go home'.

clarity bits

memnote >*at home that evening Kate was trying to understand what was really going on ... she was very curious to know how long Mac had been able to communicate ... and in how many languages*< end *memnote*

Kate You know, Mac, some moments over the last five years would have been a whole lot better had you explained what we were doing at the time and not had me figure it out for myself. I know if you could have spoken you would have, so I can only conclude that for the last couple of days we've had, 'a guest', and Mac, I do trust your judgment but ...who, what? Can I say something ... or someone ... if our 'guest' is a person I'd know ... so, do I say ghost, or what? I can tell that it means us no harm. So Casper please say something so that I can welcome you to my house?

Mac See what you have gotten me into. Why don't you do the right thing now and explain yourself?

quark >*my name is not casper ... it is quark quasar and i am not a ghost ... although i have no body with me i am here ... My body is on aGnos in suspended animation*<

Kate Suspended animation, we had a president like that. So anyway for the part of you that's here welcome to my house. I would also introduce to my dog but I figure that

	you two are online already, so how is your body anyway?
quark	>*it's fine thank you ... i'm sort of on vacation from it ... but i couldn't be if i didn't have one ... and yes Mac and i have been online for a while ... does all that make sense*<
Kate	Sort of. A bit sneaky hitting on my dog like that and why would anyone would call a planet Agnos?
quark	>*it comes out as aGnos in your language ... i couldn't explain it in mine*<
Kate	You are really lucky that I trust my dog and I know that he trusts you...otherwise...then I guess why you're here is more important at the moment than how. Do they ever call you Quacker?
quark	>*one does*<
Kate	Who?
quark	>*my boss*<
Kate	I hope he's better than mine was.
quark	>*he's a she*<
Kate	What's her name?
quark	>*eva lution*<
Kate	You're kidding, but it goes well with Agnos. What's she like?
quark	>*she's about your size ... with long hair ... don't you want to know why i'm here*<
Kate	Your boss sounded more interesting that's all; is she nice? Why does she call you Quacker?
quark	>*that's a long story ... can we get back to why i'm here*<
Kate	That's probably less interesting than discussing the fact that your boss is a

	woman. What does she do?
quark	>she is the coordinator of the Board of intergalactic Delegates<
Kate	Does she need a secretary, and what does that make you?
quark	>i'm a galactic anthropologist<
Kate	I suppose that brings us back to why you're here; speaking of hear, how come I can hear you in my head and not through my ears?
quark	>it's a part of memrec ... something like telepathy or esp ...on aGnos it's like your e-mail system ... only we can leave messages in it for others to recover at their leisure ... or it can replay an event so the listener can experience it as it happened ... think of it as a vast computer that functions on many levels and is accessible via thought ... for instance ... if you had been attacked on my planet you could have put a description of the attackers into memrec and investigators would have had a complete knowledge of the events ... not only as you described it later but as it happened ... the irony is those things don't happen on my planet<
Kate	What stops Memrec snooping?
quark	>memrec is in a way like mental graffiti ... anything someone wants to say can be addressed to memrec ... either anonymously or with the individual's unique thought signature ... there is no way it can intrude upon the individual ... because it's a receiver ... and only transmits on request ... it's also like a

mental newspaper ... it saves an awful lot of trees<

Mac   Think of that, there's actually a place where they think about saving trees. it sounds like doggie heaven.

Kate   What stops it being abused?

quark   *>intentions and attitudes ... what else<*

Kate   I guess we should get back to why you're here.

quark   *>this is a long story ... it applies to you ... not you specifically ... but all earthlings as much as me<*

Kate   If it's that long I'd better get myself a coffee. Keep talking, I can make coffee and hear you at the same time. I would offer you one but Mac doesn't drink it, but there is some water in his bowl if you're thirsty. You know that was still a pretty rotten trick you pulled using Mac like that. Are all aliens as sneaky as you?

Mac   I told you, you couldn't faze her.

quark   *>how else would you suggest i could get close enough to observe ... if i had tried to attach myself to you ... you would have sensed me immediately ... he did but couldn't tell you ... besides ... i don't control Mac ... i sort of co-exist with him ... in fact ... co-existence is something your world could experiment with to great advantage<*

Mac   if you can live with cats you can get along with anyone. Fancy, eating a mouse, YUK.

Kate   You're not wrong. Tell me, do you have coffee on Agnos? I'll never get used to that - or don't have bodies to put it in. Sorry, you told me that already.

quark	>we have bodies just like yours ... we're humanoids as well ... if i had my body with me ... i could have made the coffee and saved you the trouble ... may i continue<
Kate	It's your dime.
quark	>a hundred mergoplan years ago the governing body of the galaxy ... the G.o.d as it was known then ... made a rather stupid decision ... it allowed four planets who had been at war with each other for a thousand mergoplan years into the commonwealth ... this was on the basis that they would stop fighting each other for a period of a hundred mergoplan years ... and during that time the G.o.d would find a way ... to find a way to bring peace to mergopla ... there were many thoughts ... eventually one of our brightest prognostic evolutionists suggested that if he had the right laboratory it might be possible to evolve an essence of peace ... to this end the G.o.d needed and found a habitable planet in a small solar system that ran a hundred times faster than mergopla<
Kate	I take it, that this small fast planet is earth.
quark	>yes planet 1273<
Kate	So what happened next?
Quark	>the G.o.d beamed the personas of willing mergoplans into the aboriginal population of planet 1273 ... their mission was to learn to live with each other ... no dogma or mental impediment was sent with them ... all the participants wanted the experiment to succeed<
Kate	So, I am actually from Mergopla not Venus and I also take it that the deal is almost up,

	and you're here now to check out what happened, and to all intents and purposes the experiment failed, so what happens next?
quark	>*are you sure you don't read minds*<
Kate	I've heard my share of Sci-Fi stories.
quark	>*well ... however you guessed it ... that's the sixty zillion zoglit* [2] *question ... and the reason i have made contact with an earthling*<
Mac	Not to mention a dogling.
quark	>*including you Mac*<
Kate	When you say earthlings you seem to emphasize 'earth' and tack 'lings' on the end. Why?
quark	>*e.a.r.t.h. stands for experiment to alleviate racial tension and hatred ... apart from which because we mostly speak in thoughts our language has become less formal ...*

more intimate ... the respect you show your dog is not based on what you call him ... but on how you think of him ... you don't need to think of a capital symbol or any other attachment to his name to give the respect he deserves ... and so it should be ... beings earn respect or they don't ... titles will not give them what they don't deserve ... our language evolved away from formal status markers ... because they always seem to end up implying inequality ... so if an emphasis exists it is entirely personal like aGnos ... or it's bigger than everything like Galactic ... anyway sometimes i feel it

---

[2] z *oglit ... negotiable unit of time ... money.*

	was a pity we interfered with this place at all … but then we will never know what would have happened and there is no point ruminating over what might have been<
Kate	As an earthling I find it difficult to be so cavalier about it. You still have not told me why you stress the middle of earthling. By the way, do you know what the aborigines called it<
quark	*>by now it is probably just stress … i don't think they called it anything special … membrain may know<*
Kate	membrain? How do you spell that?
quark	*>in your language … ain not ane … he is like the collective consciousness of aGnos … a part of but separate to memrec … one of your religions would call him a being less being<*
membrain	>i resent that sir<
kate	Who was that?
quark	*>membrain … feigning offence … do you know what the aborigines of this place called it before it became<*
membrain	>there are many stories sir<
quark	*>one will do<*
membrain	>one tribe called it … great level plain between huge high mountain and big bitter water beneath vast dark twinkling sky that turns blue<
quark	*>okay okay i get the point … does that answer your question<*
Kate	Effluently … I mean fluently.
quark	*>can you agree it's a bit late to worry about what could have happened … the strange thing is … that the mergo's have*

33

	managed no matter how briefly to be more peaceful than you lot<
Mac	No one can be contrary like humans: whatever you figure, they do the opposite; at least mine is well trained.
membrain	>my sentiments exactly<
Kate	Who said that?
membrain	>i was just communicating with the k9 dear lady<
Mac	Watch it with the k9's, buddy, and my name is Mac.
Kate	Isn't this conversation going to become highly complicated if we can hear membrain talk to Mac but I can't hear anything Mac says?
quark	*>yes you two ... why don't you tick off our frequency<*
membrain	>you did invite me in sir<
quark	*>but for the moment<*
membrain	>as you wish sir<
quark	*>where were we<*
Kate	You had just told me that our ancestors are currently more dovish than us. I'll have to take your word for that but if you want my opinion the main problem has always been religion. Did you send that too, or was it a local invention?
quark	*>you would ask that ... in the first place no dogma at all was sent ... but after the initial fervor wore off ... and the descendants of the transferees started to become disruptive ... the council had to decide what to do ... eventually they sent the one you call Moses to spread a few rules around ... the first part of my report is*

	based on those rules<
Kate	How can you make an unbiased report on how well we have failed the Decalogue? if you've hung your report on that you don't need to talk to me. You've made your mind up already. By the way, if you sent Moses did you also send Jesus?
quark	*>take care … you are talking about the girl i was going to marry<*
Mac	Yeah, and I had a chance with Lassie. How's he going to explain his way out of this one?
quark	*>i heard that Mac … it means that when we sent her persona the only appropriate earthling from whom she could function happened to be a male<*
Mac	Sounds incredibly kinky to me.
membrain	>how do i file kinky sir<
Mac	I thought you'd know that... unstraight.
Kate	Am I having trouble with this communication system or did you just say that you were going to marry the one we call Jesus …
Mac	...or me a Royal Corgi.
quark	*>Mac all life is royal … some forget … that's all<*
Kate	may I ask why you didn't marry … what was her name …did you love her or is love an alien concept to aliens?
quark	*>her code name or id was dawn 2 … her real name is crystal …and i didn't marry her because when we got her back from here she was insane and has shown no signs of improvement … she doesn't even remember me … and i'm not sure what you*

mean by love ... if you mean i gave her all the freedom she needed without question and wished her all the success she wished herself ... then i loved her ... if you mean did i want to possess her and give her what i wanted her to have ... and not what she needed ... just so i could wear her as a badge and symbol of my ego and will ... then i didn't love her<

Kate   Do you still love her?

quark   >yes ... and i hate seeing her like that<

Kate   Doesn't that rather bias your report?

quark   >how do you feel about your attackers of the other night<

Kate   With all your technology, why can't you help her?

quark   >when it all started to go wrong the G.o.d couldn't make up its mind what to do ... in their defense they had no idea that things could go so wrong so quickly ... so instead of setting up constant contact they took crystal's *advice as to when they should communicate again ... and when they did it was too late to recover all of her mind before she died ... all we could do was to build her a sanctuary for as long as she wants or needs it ... we are at the stage where illness and defect is unknown ... and because our society is totally based on the individual ... no one has the right to harm one for the benefit of another ... so to find her a new persona would destroy another's ... and to clone one would raise the question of whose persona should be cloned ... if we did it for her we would have*

	to do it for others ... we can't just go around handing out reincarnation at the drop of a hat ... sometimes the best reason not to do something is because you can do it<
Mac	That's what I say to some bitches when they're on heat.
quark	*>Mac ... you're a prince<*
Kate	What do you mean by defect?
quark	*>i mean we know enough about the life process to be able to repair a potential abnormality before anyone is born<*
Kate	So you make perfect little people to fit your society?
quark	*>we do not ... we have merely built a society bereft of needless suffering ... where we allow individuals the right of dignified exit from that society if they so choose ... if crystal wanted ... she has the right to take her own existence ... however ... she has never shown any sign of wanting to ... and no one has the right to decide for her ... so she continues on beyond communication and help ... i hate it<*
Kate	What would happen if someone killed someone on Agnos?
quark	*>if not the wish of the person killed ... it would be murder and ... if proved ... the murderer forfeits all rights as an individual ... one of two things can then happen ... if the persona of the murdered person was saved ... they have the right to request reincarnation into the body of their murderer ... and the persona of their killer is allowed to dissipate ... if that is not practical or possible the murderer is asked*

to take his or her own life<

Kate   'Not the wish', and why would anyone want to be fitted into the body of the person who killed them?

quark   *>you call it euthanasia … it could be called an act of love … if Mac became incurably ill … as soon as he showed signs of discomfort … it would be considered an act of compassion to put him out of his misery<*

Mac   That's a result of the difference between Platonic and that other form of love, but there are a few old bitches who would like to see me suffer.

quark   *>surely Mac … only the unrequited<*

Kate   What if the murderer refused to go?

quark   *>our ethics allow us to make that decision … as far as a victim taking its killers body that would be very much up to the victim … might i might point out that none of these things have happened in eons<*

Kate   Can I tell you that one of the greatest contributors to the human condition was the event involving your girlfriend. Ever since murdering her, they have claimed that she died of her own free will, to save the world. I've never understood how one person's death could save the world. I can think of some who will improve it when they leave, but not actually save it. Anyway it seems from then on the idea dying for something became kosher. Anyway this report of yours, is it top secret, or are you going to let we earthlings have a look at it?

Mac   Good idea, give 'em a break. You never

know, they might just listen; a lot of dog collars have collapsed since the last time anyone tried to say anything.

quark >*can you think of any reason why they would take any notice ... if they were told why they're here*<

Mac   No I can't, but just because you can do something doesn't always mean that you shouldn't. What the hell, give it a shot.

quark >*do you know what you are suggesting ... do you have any idea of how complicated that could get*<

Mac   No more than now.

membrain   >the pooch has a point sir ... he says that if earthlings knew why they were here it couldn't make things any worse<

Mac   Go easy on that pooch stuff as well.

membrain   >allow me some alliteration please<

Kate   I find Mac's judgment sound. My life is in his care. I mean, just because you can communicate without actually speaking - understand thoughts as soon as they're formed - then place them in my brain - really, only means that yours is a higher intelligence. It doesn't prove you're Quark Quaser from a planet called Agnos. My sister, my most trusted friend, sibling, life's blood - if I tried to explain this to her she'd accuse me of sniffing glue.

quark >*so now what*<

Kate   You must have been in this situation before. What do you normally do, short of burning bushes and stuff like that? For a start can you make it possible for me to talk to Mac without involving you? I've known him for the last thirty five dog years

	and I've known you less than a day.
quark	>well membrain could network us together so that any thought from any source will be communicated to the other three<
Kate	Sounds fair.
Mac	Good: that way I can tell her the brand of dog food I want her to get.
Kate	I'm not getting that Mac, it's bad for your liver.
Mac	I knew there'd be a catch to this somehow.
quark	>Mac ... you can still have private thoughts ... you just need to learn to filter them what you want to say<
Kate	So you're saying there are open thoughts and hidden thoughts – so you can still lie?
quark	>i suppose if you would be a liar yes ... but it's more like the split between what you think and what you say ... what else can i do<
Kate	Now I know. I want to 'read' your report, with my vision in my own language. Can you arrange that?
quark	>membrain can just dump the whole thing in your mind and you will know it instantly<
Kate	I want to get it by normal means, like other people. I've been a sort of alien all my life, so if I'm amongst aliens I would like to feel like an earthling, do you understand? I want to feel that something legitimate took place, not like a one night stand that leaves you wondering what happened. Do you understand sex?
quark	>as a noun or a verb ... but i take your point ... i also have no idea how we can do

40

what you want<

Kate maybe the geek can help.   He seems to know everything.

membrain >i think she's referring to me sir<

quark *>i'm sure she is ... but i still have no idea what we can do ... my eyes are in my body on aGnos ... as such you don't use eyes ... and if we had some spare eyes ... we would still need some primitive means to produce a document for Kate to read ... and that further assumes that we have time to do all this ... which we don't<*

membrain >there's always the pooch sir<

Mac I thought we decided to cool it with the pooch stuff.

membrain >Mac you're far too sensitive ... i was going to suggest sir ... that it may be possible ... that is sir ... depending on why the girl can't see<

Kate My name is Kate, K for short, but not 'the girl' OK? And my eyes don't work because when I was born they gave me oxygen to revive me. They had no idea that too much could send a newborn blind. It happened a lot before they understood how oxygen could do that. So, tell me, how can I get to 'read' ... to 'see'... your story?

quark *>i still don't know that it's possible ... i also don't understand why you want to read it ... rather than just know it<*

Kate Because I suspect as a sort of earthly alien I already know it, but what I need to know is on what you based your opinions. It doesn't matter if I agree with you or not. The only way I can really come to know you is through your arguments. I want to see

it and read it from the beginning. is that possible, Sir?

membrain   >the girl ... I mean Kate ... has a point sir ... aGnos still maintains its written formats<

quark   *>true ... but i also know that all formal languages eventually fall victim to their cultural boundaries<*

Mac   Yeah ... when I sniff a poodle's arse I can tell if the hair do is fake, all I want to know is will my girl to be able to read your report, because if I know her, and I do, she won't let it go until she does.

membrain   >that's going to depend on you Mac ... you have the only pair of functional sense organs that will do the job<

Mac   Hey all you two noodles need to do is tell me what to do and we will do it, and I suspect, the sooner the better.

membrain   >ok Mac here's how it goes ... the aGnosics view their planet as a living organism ... and they are very interested in its health ... dogs sense and see things that homo sapiens can't ... so the aGnosic dog population contributes first line information about changes they perceive in their daily environments ... for instance ... one dog sensed ground quake conditions long before anything else ... when a dog reports an anomaly a homo sapiens can connect through me to the dog and see what it sees<

Mac   Sounds OK, but I knew a Greyhound who couldn't see anything beyond the end of his nose and even then he had to move ... and he smelt of cat hair. Where does this get us?

membrain >as usual Mac ... you cut to the bone ... through me ... Kate will use your eyes ... that way she will be able to read the report ... you will be aware of her in an out of body sort of way ... the next challenge is what she will be reading it on<

Kate What would a 'contributor' normally look at?

quark *>rarely writings<*

Kate I thought the geek ...

membrain >I can be offended too ... dear lady ... surprisingly<

Kate Sorry, membrain. Can't you just scroll it across my LCD?

quark *>that'll test your language skills membrain<*

membrain >indeed sir ... but then ... with the right approach nothing is really impossible sir<

Kate Apparently not. Look at that Mac - oh, you are already. Now all I have to remember are dad's finger lessons on the shapes of letters.

quark *>i can probably help there ... i've been here long enough to learn most of the local lingo's<*

Kate Thanks, I think, how will I know who said what?

membrain >all encoded for your convenience ma'am<

Kate Thanks again, I think?

memrec ... sector one ... level one ... code one ... transmission begins

eva	>you're off, then<
quark	*>yes, i've just been called<*
eva	>you know i've never approved of you, quark<
quark	*>wouldn't have said never<*
eva	>that's another issue ... anyway ... the council has selected you and for the sake of the mission and all concerned i'll just have to put my personal feelings aside and accept their recommendation ... you have a moment ... it won't matter if you get to there in january or half past june<
quark	*>i suppose not ... providing the vahzoom[3] operators don't mind<*
eva	>if so ... i'll explain that there are a few last minute problems ... what's the date of your arrival<
quark	*>somewhere between january and june 1899.*
eva	>i hope you've done your own research ... you're not relying on the official records to explain what happened ... and what you may find<

---

[3]*vahzoom ... device to project neural activity and the persona ... the ultimate space travel system ... developed on the trispatial theories of the great splagvoidian polyvoidaL cosmocalcula genius dr eon defsprit pcb pvc ptfe ad infinitum ... see maglusia lectubahm's book ... life and continuing time of dr eon defsprit.*

quark	*>i've spoken to a few of those involved in the operation ... i even contacted dizzy's daughter ... she said he always believed in the project but couldn't get quality volunteers<*
eva	>i called you in to remind you of crystal and to stress to you how important it is that no such thing happens again<
quark	*>i thought you'd rather enjoy that<*
eva	>that's a stupid ... callous ... and un-aGnosic thing to say<
quark	*>don't blow your orbit ... i miss her too<*
eva	>the point is that we don't need a repeat of what happened to her even if it is you<
quark	*>you would have been a terrific mother-in-law<*
eva	>sorry ... i never said being nice to you again would be easy ... the ... fractious four ... would take your death as the definitive signal the e.a.r.t.h. had failed and start up again ... they're itching anyway ... but even they have to respect the agreement and you know when that's up<
quark	*>yes all too close for comfort<*
eva	>which for us is only months so given the urgency of our situation ... i doubt there's any point in being too security conscious ... we may as well communicate direct via encrypted memcode assuming that the ... fractious four haven't cracked it ... then at least if you do fall victim to some earthly calamity i'll have your thoughts that far<
quark	*>i'll be disembodied for the duration ... they can't crucify what they can't see ... can they<*

eva	>i've heard they're very good at crucifying things sight unseen ... but i take your point<
quark	*>i guess i'd better get going the vahzoom operators will be looking for me by now ... by the way is your memcode still purple<*
eva	>why would it change ... i haven't and you're still blue<
quark	*>bye mum ... see you next year<*

poor reception

quark	*>i'm here ... mum<*
eva	>stop calling me that and get on with your job ... if the mergoplans have broken the code how do we defend a highly qualified intergalactic anthropologist calling the coordinator of the b.I.d ... mum? ... and i had enough trouble contemplating being your mother-in-law without being your mother<
quark	*>ok. ok. keep your top on<*
Kate	>am i having trouble with this communication system or did you just tell the coordinator of the b.I.d to remained clothed<
quark	*>well not exactly ... you just got the generic translation ... anyway are you going to read or pass comment<*
Kate	Probably both. How about putting those word definitions at the bottom of the 'page' so i can read them close to where they are? The next one looks like a real doozie.
membrain	>your wish is my command dear lady<
Kate	Thanks mem's.
quark	*>do you have any idea the depth of the technology going into this conversation<*
Kate	OK OK Q, I'm 'reading'.
quark	*>here's a few primary thoughts ... from my research which included all the official material on the e.a.r.t.h. and available memory records of the minor participants ... from vahzoom operators to some of the descendants of those who went*

... taking special care not to give too much credence to the media vlitzglow of the time<

eva >what are you trying to tell me<

quark *>just ... with all that preparation i'm still boggled by the beauty of this planet ... what's that mythical place the licathians believe in<*

eva >you mean the valley of vlitzium<

quark *>that's it ... well this place has to be better than that ... one would think that beauty alone would have helped the experiment along ... but instead it appears only to have given them more to squabble over ... it almost makes me believe that the G.o.d should have taken dizzy fawsett's original solution and sanctioned ... the four ... in the first place ... instead of fooling around with all this biogenic spizle<*

eva >oh quark ... you've only been there five minutes ... you can't be that negative already ... what are you going to be like in fifty years ... why don't you take a look around and talk to me again in twenty years or so ... you might have something to say that i want to hear by then<

anyone there

quark	*>if you hadn't cut me off i was going to point out that if we can pull this thing off it will vindicate dizzy's second idea... although it looks pretty hopeless at the moment ...in the last few months our time earth had a major war which wiped out about two and a half percent of the population ... all because malcontent decided kill an autocrat ... on such a violent planet you couldn't imagine one more stupid killing could bring about the of million upon millions innocents ...*
eva	>no one was ever relatively innocent<
quark	*>okay one record says that there were some fifteen million deaths ... about sixty percent of that number were directly involved ... that must mean an awful lot innocents got caught were caught in the cross fire ... however you think of that it's beyond stupid ... they called this ... the great war ... maybe because it was so terrible it just had to be great ... earthlings still refer to it as the war to end all wars ... but it didn't<*
eva	>could it still be a pubescent phase ... they're still growing<
quark	*>i don't know if they'll ever grow out of it ... i don't think they want to ... when the great war ended ... and the victors took the stage ... they based the ... new peace ... on the further punishment of their old enemy ... so not only do they lose ... they also get the booby prize for not*

winning ... this is not to say that if the tables were reversed the other side would have been any different ... but holding grudges does nothing for any one<

eva >so have they learnt anything at all<

quark *>i'm not sure how i would know<*

eva >you're the highly qualified anthropologist ... that's why you're there ... have they learnt anything ... or are they capable of learning anything<

quark *>you never know ... one minute they're quiescent and the next they're blowing each other away<*

eva >contact me when you have some evidence that they can ... can't or won't learn through their mistakes<

dispossessed

eva   >quacker ... when i said come back to me
       when you have something i didn't mean go
       silent and sulk ... and had you checked the
       date lately you'd know it's almost half past
       our safe limit ... you must have more than
       synaptic dysentery by now<

quark *>and you complain about nicknames ... you
       asked for something definitive ... the only
       thing definitive about earthlings is there's
       nothing definitive ... could almost make
       you believe in a god<*

eva   >what really reduces my orbit is that it was
       the spirit of evangelism that got us into this
       mess in the first place ... i'll never
       understand why the G.o.d took it into its
       collective head ... after thousands of years
       of quiescence ... to go on a recruiting drive
       for new members ... it should never have
       listened to that swaggering guru jimmy
       artless ... at least it's some consolation that
       he went the same way they did ... tell me
       what you've got and let's see if we can make
       something of it ... the mergo's are getting
       more restless<

quark *>it's just that ... almost immediately after
       you and i last chatted ... the great war part
       two broke out ... although to be
       fair ... more fractious factions got into the
       act and pushed hostilities further ... wider
       and longer<*

eva   >obviously they've learnt nothing<

quark	>they say they have ... there's always palaver about peace ... but you never actually see any ... even in times of so called peace ... there are underlying tensions<
eva	>and you'd know about that<
quark	>i thought we agreed to put our story aside<
eva	>just reminding you to stay alert ... and some underlying tension can be healthy<
quark	>well here it's not ... i'm never sure if the ... tension breakouts ... are local explosions ... like erupting volcanoes ... really reflect the weight of global social pressure<
eva	>it couldn't be just local ... are there places more peaceful than others<
quark	>on the surface yes ... but if you scratch ... i'm sure this whole project sounded good at the time ... but the idea may have been flawed from the beginning<
eva	>i didn't patch in to have you suggest that we're to blame for their present condition<
quark	>we interfered with their genetic code ... did we not<
eva	>you mean we gave them the chance to become great<
quark	>one memscan i infused said that due to the difficulty in raising the quota the G.o.d couldn't afford to investigate all volunteers too closely ... records show that at one time vahzoom operators went on strike ... refusing to transfer more essence of mergoplan ... because they had been told by opponents of the scheme that the essence was going into animals like dogs and cats ... causing great harm to the

entrapped personas<

eva   >quacker ... everyone knows one or two mistakes were made ... a horse received a bookie's brain<

quark   *>sounds like justice<*

eva   >for whom<

quark   *>i'm not sure ... punters<*

eva   >a whale ended up being able to speak and read four hundred languages when it received the essence of one of the greatest interpreters who ever lived ... and a number of politicians found themselves in true reptilian form ... it was finally discovered that a vahzoom bank had been sabotaged ... causing some malfunctions in the psychic aimer ... when the bookie was located to be relocated ... he refused to be moved ... he liked his life as a stallion ... the interpreter said it was great just splashing about in the ocean ... swallowing tons of krill ... so he too requested to be left alone ... as for the politicians ... no one could determine one snake from another ... so transmission resumed ... if you are going to defend them you'll have to do better than blaming their condition on randy stallions ... and the occasional white whale<

quark   *>there's more ... the G.o.d couldn't always agree<*

eva   >i should hope not ... aGnos is an etocracy[4] remember ... where ethical constructive creative argument shall always be encouraged ... what's your point ... if you can remember it<

quark   *>the results were confusing<*

eva   >i don't know that you can confuse the
       confused ... and anything to do with the
       mergos has always been confused ... that's
       why we're in this sploigel ... remember<

quark *>may i continue<*

eva   >of course ... but i hope you're taking this
       somewhere because shortly i'm doing
       visidine with the mergo delegate ... and i'm
       starting to feel grunged out on too many
       titbits already<

quark *>the first transferees were given books on
       galactic law ...*

eva   >they didn't need that sort of stuff ... what
       else<

quark *>several volumes of economic theory ...
       medical ... engineering ... and farming
       journals ...*

eva   >they didn't need that stuff either ... what
       else<

---

[4]*etocracy:* intrinsically bound to a level of living technology allowing a
society to live more on their world than from their world ...an ethical
democracy ... formed of and by a population of beings who accept
responsibility for their own existence ... as well as their co dependence
upon each other and their world ... willing to direct that responsibility
toward their mutual benefit ... as an unexclusive whole ... willing to use
imagination and creativity to remove the causes of societal disfunctionality
rather than attempt to crush ... regulate or somehow segregate thinking
into colors of 'them and us' ... a weightless user friendly envelope in which
the most important element is the individual ... not a 'me society' as such
... but rather a society of co-functioning 'me's' in which the global 'me'
recognizes the gifts of existence on a quid pro quo basis and understands
that that existence is indisputably paralleled in the health of their living
world ... without a healthy world there is no true harmony.

quark	>the *G.o.d* split over what kind of ethnic information the transferees should take with them ... and could never decide if the e.a.r.t.h. was a multicultural event ... where the guests would learn to accept and live with each other in peace ... or like each other enough to meld into one<
eva	>so ... have they<
quark	>have they what<
eva	>melded into one<
quark	>they can't even meld when they're from the same mould ... for instance ... trouble started with the children ... they began asking why were so different to the rest of the population ... their parents came up with such nonsense that many of the begotten ... began blundering about the planet trying to find themselves ... there's even evidence that some used their technology to start hybrid cultures with the primitives ... the results are still confounding modern earthlings ... so they can't cope with their own ... never mind bounding ethnic barriers<
eva	>maybe they felt the responsibility of the experiment so much that they overreacted<
quark	>as did the *G.o.d* ... all kinds of wild ideas emerged including that they should reincarnate them into new bodies at home or bring them back in their earth bodies ... nobody knew how to overcome the legal issues ... not to mention that by then ... the deep space fleet had been eliminated in favor of vahzoom projection<
eva	>surely the whole point was that they were there to learn to live with each other ...

warts and all ... and i would think that one
life after death would be enough for anyone
... and the third option<

quark

>that was to break the only rule the G.o.d
could agree on ... and inject dogma into the
experiment ... the problem was the G.o.d
had no idea how to reverse millions of years
of thought ... and afflict its own experiment
with what it knew would turn into a mania
of some sort ... it also couldn't understand
why any society wouldn't want to be
peaceful
and productive without being threatened
into it ... however ... at the insistence of
circumstances the G.o.d redefined the legal
status of the personas of the experiment to
alleviate racial tension and hatred and
forged the term ... new earthlings<

eva

>that's cute ... why not ... new aliens ... but
if we have to use it again we may as well
drop the ... new ... it's a long time since
they were fresh anything<

quark

>how can i get this report across if you keep
interrupting with trivia<

eva

>get on with it then<

quark

>this phrase implied that they had become
a separate species ... in this way the G.o.d
could sanction dogma ... memrec discloses
some of the responses of the time ... the
G.o.d abandons its own experiment to
dogma and witchcraft ... the G.o.d
sanctions voodoo ... galactic clock wound
back a billion years ...on advice from dizzy
fawsett the G.o.d gave the earth over to a
new group ... called the league of regional

delegates ... it became known as the l.o.r.d
... the l.o.r.d went looking for an individual
willing to take over the e.a.r.t.h. in its own
interests ... no aGnosics applied ... but one
well intentioned mergoplan anthropologist
named aden nibana came forward ... he
was back beamed from megalos i to earth
... on aGnos he was known as nucleus 3 ...
because some bright reporter decided that
what earth really needed was a central core
... and three was supposed to be lucky<

eva

>and you complain about me being trivial
... i knew most of that and what i didn't i
had gladly forgotten to remember ... apart
from which do you have any idea what sort
of ... job spec ... the l.o.r.d gave n3 to
follow<

quark

>i believe the term was ... left to his
abiding passion and judgment ... so if it felt
good he did it ... said it ... or acted it ...
even though he was more passion than logic
... as far as i can determine from the
fragmented memrec records he left ... he
did pretty well spreading a concept as new
to him as it was to those he was spreading
it over<

eva

>i doubt we'll go far in general discussion
... why don't you give your senses a rest
while i visidine[i] with the mergo delegate ...
we'll pick it up when i get back ... can you
devise some framework for our discussions
to speed them up ... just in case you're
wondering i'm going to have mergolusian
trout with a side salad of endalovian lettuce
beans ... sprinkled with wasmergian dulip

dust[6] ... lightly joined by a modicum of tantalanus dew[7] ... enjoy your thought break<

[5] _visidine ... to_ enjoy company and cuisine via media ... useful when one can't get home from the office to share cuisine with one's life partner.

[6] _wasmergian dulip dust ... l_ike tantalanus dew ... dulip dust starts out as a coating on a plant leaf ... but much less sweet than tantalanus dew ... and therefore counterpoints the other to perfection ... taking the sex analogy of the endalovian lettuce one step further ... dulip dust relates to tantalanus dew like a fleeting bitter sweet goodbye the day after.

[7] _tantalanus dew ..._ dew gathered from the flame colored leaves of the tantalanus bush ...some observers insist that the bush appears to be on fire ... dew exuded from the leaves is unlike any other ... it is agreed that if the dew is collected just before dawn and held in a neutral non reactive light tight vessel for 90 earth days ... an enzyme leached from the tantalanus leaf by the dew converts the dew into the most excruciatingly glorious rounded champagne ... when this champagne is used as spice it brings the most remarkable flavor to any thing at all.

flexitime

quark	*>are you done with visidine yet ... i hope your fish was off ... what a terrible thing to tell someone whose body lies in a suspended animation tank ... with nutrient tubes up its nose<*
eva	>no need to pout ... i looked in on it the other day ... you know ... it looks cute when you're not in it<
quark	*>you're sweet too ... i suspect it won't want to know me when i get back to it ... how is the mergoplan delegate today ... dull i hope ... or expired<*
eva	>the fish was wonderful and the delegate could have been more delicate in essence ... excuse the pun ... he said that mergopla was ready for anything ... so what's your plot to conserve the cosmos<
quark	*>how about we just discuss n3's rules ... and see what happens ... in case you don't know them the second one is...*
eva	>thou shalt not make any graven image ... or any likeness of anything that is in heaven above ... or that is in the beneath ... or that is in the waters beneath the earth<
quark	*>how come you know that<*
eva	>i accessed n3's memfile so we could bite on the same bits<
quark	*>very punny ... i think he should have made it the first rule ... it would have been better to start with a strong statement and then explain why it was made and how ... if it were followed ... it would benefit all*

59

	earthlings ... not just the few he foisted them on<
eva	>how was he sent there<
quark	*>you pulled his file<*
eva	>you'll have to allow me to ask the obvious now and again ... so how<
quark	*>ok ... ok ... via vahzoom projection ... he was back beamed from megalos2 ... i told you ... he occupied a suitable host ... his body languished in a tank ... like mine does now ... and he was put into a baby for logistical reasons ... there was something strange there though ... he was supposed to be returned to his body ... no one knows what happened to it but his body was lost in storage ... so he was never returned<*
eva	>then he was planet bound when he got there and senseless until he did ... where did he conceive all that stuff ... if one follows his thinking he is describing a point below the heaven above ... and above the below ... and above the water below that ... so where was he ... a thousand meters above ground ... two thousand or twenty two thousand ... did he have an allergy toward his host that unbalanced his senses<
quark	*>possibly ... he was just trying to describe the biggest space he thought the natives could get their brains around ... because he goes on to say that they shouldn't make images out of anything found in that general area ... seeing that his supreme being built all the stuff in between and he would be offended if he caught them taking*

happy snaps ... as it is ... a vast number of
earthlings believe their god created the
earth ... and them ... and everything else
for that matter ... on what seems to be
some form of broadband flexitime in seven
days ... including one of rest and
recuperation for good behavior<

eva >that's stupid ... he was supposed to un-
confuse them ... not compound their
problems ... surely he was trying to say
more than that ... what if a woman wanted
her mate to bring home a house cat to kill
the rats eating her grain ... and to stop him
coming back with a slavering great beast
she carves a little pussy to explain what
she wants ... according to this rule she
would be doing something wrong<

quark *>i gather n3 was warning them about*
carving images as esoteric and mystic
experiences and then attributing strange
powers to them<

eva >so he was trying to channel their desire
for mystic experiences toward a dialogue
with his newly invented   supreme being ...
wasn't such a super being harder for them
to cope with than a little deity for every
disaster<

quark *>i think that's why he left them with ...*
dominion ... over the planet ... but also
planted the idea that no matter how
powerful they became there was someone
stronger<

eva >his great supreme<

quark *>of course<*

eva >but you keep telling me they show no sign

of being in charge of themselves ... i can't fathom what n3 was on about when he did such an extravagantly stupid thing ... if he had been thinking clearly he would have appealed to their business acumen ... they are ex-mergos after all ... he could have explained that running one god would be cheaper than a dozen ... or point out there'd be no value in praying for help to a product of the same evolution that had produced them ... this would have to be an example of the stupid lauding the insensible<

quark   >*no doubt his efforts were aggravated by the fact that the principles he was trying to refresh had de-evolved from their experience*<

eva   >why didn't he just tell them who they were ... where they were from and what they were doing there<

quark   >*maybe he thought that that would lead to them opt out completely and start some star gazing cult*<

eva   >what if they were to live a thousand years and be forced to live through the results of their shortsightedness ... then they would be forced to take a responsible view of time ... albeit only for their own comfort and survival<

quark   >*they would probably decide they had so much time it wouldn't matter what happened ... it gets us no closer to making them understand that the future is the hapless victim of the present ... and time is more than an unending parade of seasons ... moons or sidereal sequences arranged for their amusement and pleasure*<

eva	>how many rules did n3 invent for this great supremo to give to them<
quark	*>rumor reports that there were originally twelve but he broke a couple getting them down off the mountain<*
eva	>what were they ... thou shalt learn to live with each other ... and thou shalt not be miserable ... pity he hadn't broken all of them ... what's the next one ... and what's photography got to do with anything<

spare ribs

quark   >are you ready for this<
eva   >about as keen as i am to know the
         mergoplan delegate's sperm count<
quark   >thou shalt not worship any deity or idol
         but God ... what does that suggest to you<
eva   >it was written by the mergoplan delegate<
quark   >no ... when n3 took the stops out and
         made G.o.d into God ... and then demanded
         that its followers provide it with absolute
         faith or else ... he had no idea whether he
         wanted them to think of his God as an all
         powerful ... all pervading deity ... or just
         another little graven image like those he
         was trying to stamp out with his first rule<
eva   >so where shall we put the emphasis ...
         with the stops ... it was on the first symbol
         ... it means nothing to me without the stops
         ... shall we just call it god ... apart from
         which you're saying he was confused ... on
         the one hand he had to provide them with a
         tool to move forward and on the other ...
         worshipping anything was outside his
         experience ... he possibly thought anything
         would be better than nothing<
quark   >whatever his logic ... gods are everywhere
         and they even have a devil<
eva   >what's a devil<
quark   >now that is confusing ... you're a little
         devil aren't you ... is used as a term of
         endearment ... generally at the very young
          or very old to excuse some sort of behavior
         that in an adult earthling would be

64

	offensive ... irritating or criminal<
eva	>that's a real devil<
quark	*>no ... the real devil ... or satan ... as generally named is the anti-god ... the evil one ... the supreme who resides over hell ... also called hades ... where the sinners ... or non-repentants go when they die ... good people and those who have repented their sins go to heaven and have eternal life ... or so they believe<*
eva	>how about selecting their main three gods to tell me about ... we're going to be out of real time aGnos the way this is going<
quark	*>three is limiting ... many things are godlike to them<.*
eva	>name four <
quark	*>food ... sex ... money ... power ... oil<*
eva	>five ... mmmm ... sex can be limiting ... loving is better ... food can be over done ... money ... can be a problem anywhere ... pursuing power can be negative and is why they were sent there in the first place ... so now what ... any thoughts<
quark	*>well ... maybe ... all their examples of power have a dark side ... one of their myths is that their definitive god created Adam ... the first man ... then he gave him a garden to tend and animals to name ... but one day the god decided Adam needed a helper of his own ...*
eva	>i know this one ... what's your angle<
quark	*>the god cloned the woman from adam's spare rib ... obviously spare because no man seems to suffer ill by its loss<*
eva	>have you been playing near strong

	magnetic fields by any chance<
quark	>*upon my frequency i haven't ... but it shows you how complicated they are to have a god so devious as to clone the first woman out of a component of the first man ... making them brother and sister ... no wonder it took a serpent ... the devil ... with an apple to corrupt this perfect existence*<
eva	i know about the apple ... what did the serpent actually do with it<
quark	>*fed it to eve ... who in turn conned Adam into nibbling on a bit ...*
eva	>of it ... or her<
quark	>*the former ... which led to the latter ... when their god discovered them munching on his delicious apples he became very bitter ... demanding to know why they'd broken one of his rules ... adam said she'd given it to him ... the woman ... eve ... accused the serpent of beguiling her ... their god said he didn't much care where it came from because he knew where they were going ... he then evicted them from the garden of eden to suffer the wilderness outside*<
eva	>that's sweet ... blame it on the girls ... and i've heard woman was given cellulite as well ... was n3 a male chauvinist ... surely such a supremo could have cooked up woman without a recipe leading to incest ... i can believe anything of them now ... how can nations get on when males and females can't<
quark	>*maybe the point here is that even their first experiences with powerful entities*

create vengeance cycles ... their god got angry over the apple thing ... apparently completely forgetting its part in constructing eve from adam's rib ... there was no duty of care demonstrated by the god at all ... no instructions as to the care of and avoidance of eating apples proffered by serpents ... and if the serpent was sent by the god to test them ... it shows a very nasty streak for any being ... not to mention the supposedly supreme one ... it all seems to go rather well with the ...up you i'm fine syndrome ... that leads to power hungry freaks trying to model the world in their own image<

eva   >who knows ... maybe the devil made him do it ... but i get your drift ... they have no real example of power for individual good ... are we done on that subject ... what's next<

quark   >name it<

eva   >as i said ... sex can be limiting ... loving is better ... discussing either won't get us much further now ... let's stop for thought break<

going home

quark	*>thou shalt not take the name of the lord thy god in vain ... for the lord will not hold him guiltless that taketh his name in vain<*
eva	>sounds paranoid to me ... first it's no other god but me ... now it's don't put sploigel on my name ... and ... another thing ... the l.o.r.d or the G.o.d weren't going to pop down to earth and punish anyone ... that was never the plot ... if misrepresentation can be called ... in vain ... maybe n3 is guilty as well ... so how does this turn out<
quark	*>well ... you sort of ... cut to the chase ahead of time<*
eva	>that's why i'm the coordinator and you're the anthropologist ... sorry ... i guess we have to deal with the downstream and not the source ... so what happened then ... after<
quark	*>it's certainly a threat and it certainly gave rise to a strange pattern of behavior in their relationship to their god ... by the way ... i like to think of their god as female ... t here's something rather blonde about the way they view their god<*
eva	>blonde<
quark	*>blondes are supposed to be dumb ...air heads ... as the expression goes ... but at the same time they credit her with creating existence ...in seven days i might add ... so she can't be all that dumb ... can she ... that reminds me how was the*

	undersec ... is it still the lady from agnoid 4<
eva	>perturbed ... and yes<
quark	*>you know ... on this planet they would say that she was Chinese and they would call you a Negro ... why is she perturbed<*
eva	>there's a rumor about a new mergoplan weapon of mass destruction<
quark	*>there've been rumblings for years but nothing has ever blown up ... erk ... scuse the pun ...what's it supposed to be<*
eva	>i don't know enough to discuss it ... particularly long distance ... so where are we going with all this name in vain stuff<
quark	*>n3's ideas ... commandments ... have become the core of a whole range of popular dogmas called religions ... through which earthlings pass the final responsibility for their condition over to their god<*
eva	>if there was a supermarket for deities where life forms could browse what are the qualities they would look for in a god<
quark	*>dumb ... very dumb ... but they would want her to have sufficient power to create them ... the planet and everything on it ... but not enough interest to care what happens to it after they'd taken possession of it ... but still love and look after their souls after death and hope for everlasting life in heaven like a five star hotel that goes on forever and ever ... amen<*
eva	>amen to you ... too ... you must admit ... it's a wonderful concept<
quark	*>it's worse than that ... having a god*

empowers them ... enables individuals or groups to act as they please saying that their authority is so high that it overrides everything else ... so it becomes okay for one faction to terrorize another if their beliefs differ ... for as they see it they're doing their god's work by removing non-believers or brainwashing new converts<

eva   >let's get back to the souls ... where did the idea of souls in heaven come from in the first place ... did n3 ever imply it in any of his rules<

quark   *>no ... it's their own invention ... and if they don't get up to heaven for a good time ... they go down to hell to be punished by the devil ... in an ocean of sploigel where a stiff lower lip is the difference between ...*

eva   >yes ... yes ... i get the idea ... it also sounds like a beauty treatment i heard about once ... what sort of behavior would direct an earthling towards hell<

quark   *>heresy for one ... believers were branded heretics if they expressed a slightly changed view ... at one time it was heresy to say that the planet was round when everyone knew it was flat ... if you went too far you fell off the edge<*

eva   >i presume they're through their flat earth phase ... so now what sort of behavior rates a ticket to their devil's playground now<

quark   *>hard to say ... i suspect that the biased and gifted who spend a lot of time praying to the god ... believe that all those who don't will go straight to hell<*

eva   >so who decides who goes to heaven or hell<

quark	>godocrats ... religious industry workers who interpret their god's words for the masses to digest<
eva	>you're saying that n3's rules have become an industry ... so are there many different products<
quark	>the product is always the same ... heaven and how to get there ... and there is a lot of competition in the market between carriers for business<
eva	>you mean this godocracy thing has become a power base with contractors competing for souls as it were<
quark	>its worse than that ... because as there's no evidence that their god ever says anything on its own ... the godocrats have total power over how their ... ceo ... is perceived by the masses ... and what the masses should do to stay in her good books<
eva	>good books<
quark	>they believe she knows everything about everyone on the planet and records it to be used on judgment day ... when the spirit of the recently deceased arrives at the pearly gates of heaven<
eva	>pearly gates ... sounds like the valley of vlitzium to me ... any way ... i think we've done this ... although i still don't know where the in vain thing starts and stops ... i suspect there is sufficient potential for complaint between what the godocrats say their god is all about ... and what it has become clear that their god is not about ... to cause considerable name taking in vain<
quark	>maybe all n3 meant was that they shouldn't call upon their god needlessly ...

like the boy who cried cribblevang[8] ... and look to their own resources for solutions within the context of the other nine rules ... by doing so they become self reliant and move away from any habitual need of an almighty to fend for them at all ... then one day they may be able to accept the responsibility of their own actions without taking their lord's name in vain as it were<

eva   >is that it<

quark   *>for the moment<*

eva   >hmmm ... well ... as we used to say on the doggy G.o.d show<

quark   *>i know ... don't call me ... i'll call you<*

[8] _cribblevang_ ... *mythical creature of the planet marithia, believed capable of changing from one form to another ... its favored form was always the one it wasn't in at any particular time ... it therefore spent most of its time in a state of confusion ... legend states that if one could capture and hold a cribblevang in any of its forms it would grant its captor three wishes ... there is an entire zoological exhibit on marithia not devoted to the cribblevang ... but to those who spent their lifetimes hunting it ... it seems they all suffered from delusions ... migraines and various forms of untreatable psychoses ... death in all cases was due to cirrhosis of the liver ...*

bingo

eva	>off your can slacko<
quark	*>for a moment i thought your showbiz rain check had become a permanent condition ... but i see that you've been de-digitizing my garbage file ... why for the bugle blast<*
eva	>thought you might be offended if i ignored your subscript ... besides ... the mergos are stepping up their campaign to discredit the e.a.r.t.h. ... by innuendo if by no other means ... i've had mem meetings with all the council members as well as that splazelbrain mergo delegate ker bajim<
quark	*>what's he on about this time<*
eva	>he was trying to discover if we had any recent intelligence on the e.a.r.t.h. that would complement his own high expectations<
quark	*>he's a politician is he not ... how would he cognize intelligence it if he fell on it<*
eva	>actually ... more like a poly-tician because i've heard it all before<
quark	*>no doubt you gave him an old showbiz reply<*
eva	>something like that ... what's next<
quark	*>rule four<*
eva	>oh yes ... six days shalt thou labor and do all thy work ... but on the seventh day is the sabbath of the lord thy god ... in it thou shalt not do any work ... thou ... nor thy son ... nor thy maidservant ... nor thine ox ... nor thine ass ... nor any of thy cattle ... nor thy stranger that is within thy

gates ... that thy manservant and thy maidservant may rest as well as thou ... i'd have a care with this one if i were you<

quark
>*i gather your meeting with ker bajim was not as dismissible as you first implied*<

eva
>he is the most forgettable male i know ... and you'll be the second if you refer to him again<

quark
>*presumably all the before mentioned were going to eat on the sabbath ... that means that someone had to work in the kitchen ... it may also be presumed that the rule is addressed to the male of the house ... as it mentions only male things ... such as oxen and cattle ... and there is a son ... now unless the addressee obtained that son by adoption or miracle ... he must have a female around somewhere ... so may we conclude that it is the woman who will work on the sabbath ... to prepare a meal for what could be a house guest ... a husband and son ... possibly even a daughter who didn't rate a mention ... not to mention the manservant and for some strange reason the maidservant ... who ... all ...incidentally ... are supposed to have the sabbath off*<

eva
>it all sounds like mini minded chauvinism to me ... what if the female gives birth on the sabbath ... that's hard labor ... would the male then forbid his woman so to do<

quark
>*the problem i see is that n3 didn't define what he meant by work ... their god looked out over limitless under developed space and decided to fill it with infinite stars ...*

planets ... meteors ... comets ... asteroids
... moons ... black holes ... suns etcetera in
six hitherto unknown earth days<

eva   >you can't suggest that preparing meals for
husband and itinerant guests isn't working
... and if someone didn't go out and milk
the goat on the sabbath it wouldn't be
working ... just loafing around the lower
forty<

quark   *>lower forty<*

eva   >don't tell me you haven't infused your own
garbage file<

quark   *>earlier on ... you said something about the*
obvious<

eva   >so i did ... i'm beginning to think that n3's
rules are too complicated to observe<

quark   *>if the observers are going to be manual*
workers they are ... but if they're going to
be the upper crust ... and employ
nonbelievers to work for them on the
sabbath it might work<

eva   >that just sounds like the beginning of
another sectarian group to me ... surely
n3's job was to integrate ... not segregate<

quark   *>true ... but given all that ... and the fact*
that ministers ... priests ... and rabbis ...
etcetera work on the sabbath ... is it any
wonder they remain confused about it ...
and still not wholly agreed on what day all
of the above was supposed to transpire ...
some think it's what they call saturday ...
others think it's sunday ... saturday is the
end of the previous week and sunday is the
beginning of the coming week ... so by
inference they don't know if their god

	rested before he started or after he finished<
eva	>i had no idea gods took holidays ... like it or not ... after every genesis they have to take a break ... like giving birth is a break from pregnancy<
quark	*>given that example<*
eva	>pregnancy<
quark	*>no ... the god rested idea ... some earthlings rest so well before they begin they in fact never do ... while others rest after they finish to the point that they forget why and what they started ... the result is that some of the community never get to talk to others ... because on the day it's legal for one to talk ... it's not legal for the other to listen<*
eva	>trust them to be literal when it suits ... i wonder what their god does on their sabbath<
quark	>apparently while they're putting in their orders for the rest of the week ... their god spends a lot of time hanging out in bingo halls ... dog tracks ... and golf courses ... just to keep up with the faithful<
eva	>dare i ask ... what is bingo halls<
quark	*>bingo ... is a game modeled on the heavenly number system ... they get together in halls to play bingo<*
eva	>you've been there too long<
quark	*>long enough ... they believe that when god calls their number ... they have to go<*
eva	>go where<
quark	*>hopefully ... heaven<*
eva	>of course ... not hell ... that's why they go

	to church and pray ... and dog tracks<
quark	*>their god is everywhere<*
eva	>where would their god find the most followers on the sabbath<
quark	*>there are so many possibilities ...*
eva	>running out of time ... just pick one<
quark	*>for spectators or players<*
eva	>players<
quark	*>right ... the golf course <*
eva	>golf as a word ... like so many of theirs conveys zut all as to what it means<
quark	*>in golf the player a little white ball around a specially maintained field perforated with eighteen holes ... it's so complicated that even highly skilled professionals have trouble playing it with the same degree of proficiency twice ... and are paid large sums of money when they do ... golf was invented by a highland group whose male folk wear a dress called a kilt<*
eva	>by choice<
quark	*>apparently<*
eva	>wouldn't that be confusing<
quark	*>no more than women wearing trousers<*
eva	>maybe it's the answer to their chauvinism<
quark	*>i doubt that ... there's no evidence that the kilt set is any better than the others<*
eva	>do females play golf<
quark	*>some males ... if asked ... would explain that that's why golf courses have little signs on them saying ... replace all divots ... they're the dividends of clobbering more bent than ball<*
eva	>what's bent<

quark	>*other than a golf club used for digging ... bent is a grass used on golf courses*<
eva	>i gather girls clobber more bent than boys ... or is it just more chauvinism<
quark	>*most players start out as gardeners ... some get better ... some don't*<
eva	>do girl gardeners get more stick than boy gardeners while they are learning to do better<
quark	>*the mergoplan delegate really straightened your curls didn't he ... why are we harping on about chauvinism*<
eva	>it's the concept ... god is superior but we are superior for having one ... and closing the argument by perverting the relationship further by feminizing it ... so the male decision makers claim further superiority by thinking of their god as blonde<
quark	>*where did that get us*<
eva	>you said you thought of their god as female because of the blonde view ...
quark	>*golf isn't the only sport to achieve religion status and so be worshipped and prayed for on the sabbath ... there's also tennis*<
eva	>tennis ... another one that gives no clue to what it is ... zlooming ... now that symbol suggests motion ... so what is tennis<
quark	>*another game ... another white ball ... and it appears to the observer that the players try to dispose of this ball ... this one soft and furry about the size of a gibelobian grape[9] ... by knocking it back and forth across a small field ... the object of the game ... apart from mass marketing of high lifestyle merchandise ... is to get the ball*

past the other player ... thusly making
points ... to keep score they use funny
language like thirty/fifteen ... deuce ... let
... ace ... love ... which in this case ...as in
many others ...means zut all<

eva   >you should talk<

quark   >i believe you and i have an agreement<

eva   >so did i<

quark   >tennis ... golf ... football ... cricket ...

eva   >i know cricket ... a small insect that keeps
you awake on hot nights when you're
camping out<

quark   >cricket ... your excellency ... is yet another
game ... another ball ... another field ... it's
so indescribably complex that a particular
sector of earthlings used it to found the
greatest empire in modern times ... the
logic seeming to be that if the enemy could
be confounded into learning how to play
cricket ... they'd be benign for years ... and
if they ever mastered it they'd be just as
twisted as their colonists ...and both would
get along famously<

eva   >should we try it on the mergoplans<

---

[9]gibelobian grape ... the most perfect vitamin supplement of any known
galaxy ...it also makes the most delightful wine known ... with a light and
delicate nose ... reputedly something like the perfume one gets from
collecting the dew from forty million glotsem petals.
glotsem ... a tree not unlike a willow but flower bearing ... sometimes used
to make ceremonial veils for fervid bridal rites.

quark	>*doubtful the mergos would respond ... but earthlings relate to that kind of worship because they made up the rules ... and understand the play ... and don't have to await the determinations of a divine umpire*<
eva	>well i guess that's bingo ... i have to go now so i'll engage my brainclone and reload later<

doubt and dishonor

quark   >are you there or do i have to leave it with membrain<

eva=bc   >that's a dumb question ... how would you know if wasn't here to answer it<

quark   >i would presume that you had left a message with membrain who would tell me that you weren't there to respond ... so he would instead<

eva=bc   >so why not ask membrain in the first place<

quark   >because you may be offended if i ignored the possibility that you were there to respond ... besides when eva left me to communicate with her brainclone ... i thought it would always be there<

eva=bc   >i am not an it ... i am a virtual independent conscious extension of the unconscious mind of eva ... i act as if the physical eva was present ... and to think billions of hours went into developing the technology we are now using for this conversation<

quark   >you are offended<

eva=bc   >what's next<

quark   >honor thy father and thy mother as the lord thy god hath commanded thee ... that thy days may be prolonged ... and that it may go well with thee in the land which the lord thy god giveth thee ...the problem here is that unlike animals earthlings don't need to do anything special to procreate ... some fish have to swim up river rapids to the

place of their own hatching to start a new
generation ... there are turtles who haul
themselves with limbs unsuited to the task
...up the beach of their own birth to lay the
embryos of next generation in the sand<

eva=bc   >aren't earthlings animals as well<

quark   >you are being pedantic<

eva=bc   >you didn't say ... unlike other animals ...
you seem to have a bit of attitude
happening there ... i would query eva<

quark   >alright ... alright ... compared to other
animals ... by the way ... i'm the one whose
body is in a suspended animation tank with
tubes up its nose<

eva=bc   >don't tell me your problems ... i'm only a
volume of brain patterns rooted in evas'
unconscious and captured in a vapour
chamber ... so any opinion i may express
would be past tense ... apart from which i
am all eva up to twenty minutes ago ... so
can we get on<

quark   >i'm trying to explain is that earthlings
beget life without concern for geography ...
season or special conditions<

eva=bc   >like other homo sapiens worlds<

quark   >yes ... so they take life as being fairly
cheap<

eva=bc   >earthlings not homo sapiens<

quark   >the result is that like everything else on
this planet parenthood means different
things to different earthlings ... some
consider it an inconvenience in the extreme
to be bowed down with little creatures
requiring help with every function from the
putting in of food ... and taking away of

82

what used to be food ... to its personal hygiene ... to be bothered starting the process in the first place ... others ... however ... shouldn't be allowed within procreating distance of each other ... for the resulting unions are less than happy ... and the little earthling born of and into these circumstances may be commencing a life that will be anything but good ... for no reason or fault of his or her own<

eva=bc   >should they have a test to determine who should be<

quark   *>be what<*

eva=bc   >allowed within<

quark   *>that would be undemocratic<*

eva=bc   >eva thinks democracy began at home<

quark   *>only in democracies ... besides ... if the hapless little chap pointed out the fact that he didn't ask to be born ... he'd be told that no one in the planet's history had ever been consulted over the nature of their birth ... he'd have to take his chances like everyone else ... i suppose it's doubtful whether the little turtle scurrying down the beach to the sea remembers asking his mother to produce him ... if turtles can and do ponder such points<*

eva=bc   >you suggest earthlings should give such matters more thought than turtles ... no matter how hard it is to flop up a beach on flippers<

quark   *>what about the situation where the child isn't wanted by either parent and made to feel like an alien in its own family ... they may not be worth honoring ... it could have* said ...honor they who are honorable ... and given a short explanation of what it considered honorable ... but no ... he says honor someone because of position and that's it ... i mean the old man may be an axe murderer<

eva=bc >i take that to mean a man who uses an axe as a murder weapon ... and not a man who kills axes<

quark >i know ... i know ... i've been here too long and lapse into journalese ... and you're still being pedantic<

eva=bc >i also suspect the lowest form<

quark >there is no lowest form of journalese ... like an axe is an axe and a murderer is a murderer and the old woman may have driven him to it ... so should the son or the daughter admire the way the old boy boogied his blade ... n3 has further confused them by connecting honor with longevity ... did he mean that if an earthling didn't follow his father's advice he may die young ... this begs the question of what the father knew of longevity<

eva=bc >you mean ... other than having some himself ... i think he meant experience<

quark >as in how to swing an axe<

eva=bc >hopefully more passively ... and from a wider range than just personal<

quark >now you're swinging it ... possibly because n3 didn't understand it himself ... he added as a bribe that this honoring will help things to go well in the land which the lord thy god hath given thee ... apart from casting their god in the role of a real estate

agent ... a quality no agent has enjoyed
since ... it doesn't explain the connection
between longevity and parental advice<

eva=bc >possibly quoting the child ... in that all
parental advice takes too long ... therefore
has something to do with longevity<

quark >very droll ... and he didn't venture his
opinion as to what parenting might be ...
and ignored other forms of parenthood ...
like father of his country ... the car ... flight
... the jet engine ... and so on ... the list is
long and impressive ... if you happen to be
an earthling<

eva=bc >your examples are hardly relevant to the
time of n3 but i understand what you mean
... they also all seem to be
male same sex virgin births ... why is that<

quark >not sure they're all virgin ... i'm quite sure
the ... father of his country ... managed to
interact with more than his share of virgins
along the way ... there is one ... necessity is
the mother of invention<

eva=bc >other than necessity ... why are they all
masculine ... is it that they don't think
enough of their females to list them as
equal ... are you sure that sexual conflict
isn't their main problem<

quark >they've never actually drawn battle lines
and retreated into opposite corners ... but
skirmishes do occur ... the most notable
was over the emancipation of females<

eva=bc >meaning<

quark >giving them the vote<

eva=bc >apparently they couldn't even do that
without rubbing it in<

quark	>how so<
eva=bc	>well if the females had given the males the vote would they have been effeminated<
quark	>i suppose not<
eva=bc	>so the sexes only really fraternize on a part-time basis ... how do they expect to resolve broader issues when they can't even come to terms with biology<
quark	>it's more than that ... they have placed biology between them and resolving those differences ... some tribes kill their own daughters if they fraternize with unacceptable others<
eva=bc	>murder above dishonor ... surely parenthood is all about love and understanding ... so how does parenthood stand as a unit when they exploit rather than diminish the differences between the sexes<
quark	>more like a triangle than a circle ... but it's not all bad ... most earthlings think highly of their parents and follow their footsteps in one way or another ... doctors follow doctors ... lawyers follow lawyers ... thieves follow thieves ... or is it lawyers follow thieves<
eva=bc	>surely that's another report<
quark	>don't get snippy ... just trying to lighten the mood<
eva=bc	>sorry ... but in the face of a problem of pan-galactic proportions we need more than trivia ... and something less tragic than some of them are willing to kill their own to save face<

quark	*>what did you tell me before ... why not ask membrain in the first place ... we have to ask the questions don't we ... or we'd be as bad as this mob shooting from the hip at the drop of an autocrat<*
eva=bc	>you have ten minutes to finish ... because i have a meeting with ker bajim and eva<
quark	*>since when do brainclones go to meetings like that<*
eva=bc	>since the mergoplans started throwing their diplomatic weight around ... and eva has to be in four brainplanes at once<
quark	*>maybe this parenthood thing is simpler than we think<*
eva=bc	>you have eight minutes<
quark	*>there are creationists and evolutionists ... the creationists believe that they are perfect models of their god the creator ... they have closed minds and believe there is nothing else to learn ... then there are the evolutionists who believe that they are the product of natural selection and evolution over millions of years<*
eva=bc	>you have seven minutes ... come to the point please<
quark	*>the creationists feel perfectly legitimate in that their gene pool comes direct from their god ... and they despise the evolutionists because they believe that Homo sapiens evolved from a monkey-like creature ... who is no longer with them ...*
eva=bc	... and where does that get us<
quark	*>i don't know ... but i suspect that the creationists are pissed of ... because they have more than a sneaking suspicion that the evolutionists are right<*

87

eva=bc   >so you are saying that those who are trapped in a belief cycle that disallows them to believe in evolution ... are really angry about being wrong and resent the evolutionists ... how does that help us with the e.a.r.t.h.<

quark   *>in the big picture it makes the earthling family dysfunctional<*

eva=bc   >maybe they don't even care ... and it's an excuse to form a mono structure they can use as a power base ... to think i turned down being the Dog-head presenter on the doggy G.o.d show ... you now have no minutes left<

escape

eva	>what's this one about quacker<
quark	*>you're back<*
eva	>i said i would ... how was my bc<
quark	*>snippy ... what mood were you in when you modeled her<*
eva	>i wasn't dreaming of a cosy b&b with my lover ... can we get on<
quark	*>ok ... ok ... thou shalt not desire thy neighbor's wife ... neither shalt thou covet thy neighbor's house ... his field ... or his manservant ... or his maid servant ... his ox ... or his ass ... or anything of thy neighbor<*
eva	>shock treatment perhaps<
quark	*>possibly he meant that a maid was worth coveting ... whereas a wife was only worth desiring<*
eva	>wouldn't this depend on the females in particular<
quark	*>more like the male in question<*
eva	>probably<
quark	*>assuming the mistress was to follow the same rule ... it goes without saying that she could not be desired by her husband's manservant ... but she had to not covet him ... and depending upon her sexual preferences she could not be desired by her husband's maid ... but again she had to not covet her in return ... and his manservant could only not covet his boss's maid servant<*

eva	>okay ... okay ... one would have to be starbribian judge to figure out all its implications<
quark	*>it also means ... taking the wife as the reader that she is not allowed to covet anything that is her husband's ... such as his house or his ox ... why she'd want his ox i don't know<*
eva	>maybe for soup<
quark	*>she is also not allowed to covet his ass ... this means different things to different people ... but i presume it relates to personal transport<*
eva	>could be the same thing<
quark	*>you don't need to remind me that you worked your way through delegates' school as a scriptwriter on the doggy G.o.d ... and she wasn't to covet anything else her husband owned ... no doubt including herself ... now that wouldn't go well in earth's twenty-first century ... for a wife owns half her husband's property ... and in case of divorce the court decides what of the rest she'll get ... so she doesn't have to covet his anything ... the law will do that for her ... as far as his ox is concerned ... the farmer's wife gets her half of the tractor and his oxen ... but she will probably let him keep his ass<*
eva	>you mean the other one<
quark	*>assuredly ... she could even apply for his maidservant if she felt so inclined ... to have someone look after the children ... her husband would get to keep the manservant ... if he so chose ... of course if this situation came about because her husband*

found solace by coveting his maidservant ...
his wife might not feel very charitable
toward him and take his ass as well<

eva   >no doubt the other one<

quark   >we can only assume that they should
never have listened to freud<

eva   >yes ... what is freud<

quark   >sigmund freud ... the father of modern
psychology ... he spent his life trying to
explain them to themselves ... and to
himself<

eva   >did he succeed<

quark   >he couldn't get all of his apostles to agree
... never mind the rest of the planet ... if he
had i'd be home by now ... however... he did
manage to confuse them into thinking that
they were unconfused ... and now the most
expensive friend an earthling can have is
his shrink<

eva   >brain trainer<

quark   >i have enough trouble with their slang
without you inventing more<

eva   >how did he confuse them into un-
confusion<

quark   >he based much of his logic on the premise
that all earthling behavior has a sexual
core ... the male child competes with the
father for the mother's affection ... and the
female child does the same for the father's
affection<

eva   >i should imagine that even the dumbest
contestant on the doggie G.o.d show would
have known that<

quark   >i didn't say that he knew what he was
talking about ... but neither did n3 ...

because taking the first part ... about desiring a neighbor's wife ... n3 says nothing about who ... thou ... is ... thou ... could be male or female of any species ... it says nothing of what desire means ... to talk to her ... request her assistance ... look at her ... listen to her ... help her ... or desire her to be happy ... there are many things that the reader of this rule could desire for his neighbor's wife ... without wanting to ... know ... her<

eva   >as i understand it ... when n3 gave them this rule wifedom was somewhat one dimensional<

quark   *>that's true and earthlings being what they are ... in some places wives are still possessions ... in the better bits ... wives are full and free partners<*

eva   >how about telling it to membrain now ... i've got a visitor<

quark   *>what's happened to your brainclone<*

eva   >she's doing visidine with the androplan delegate's alter ego<

quark   *>alright i'm going<*

memnote   *>code one ... level one ... sector one ... the following is marked ... release to braincode only ... attention eva lution<* end memnote

membrain   >back again are we sir ... oh i'm still checking what i've forgotten ... to find out when i was surprised ... it's taking so much longer than i'd thought<

quark   *>please don't boggle your bio-chips<*

membrain   >thank you sir<

quark >*report continues ... this rule in any time can only be considered sexist ... for it says nothing about a wife desiring another male ... or female and is not to say that a bride considers a future time when she may be attracted to another ... for both bride and groom are programmed to be deliriously happy with nothing further from their minds*<

membrain >indeed sir ... did you know that one of the smaller planets of the connubia complex ... even started a honeymoon haven on one of its moons ...   their slogan was ... save money ... make your honey on our moon<

quark >*well ... as what passes for life on earth has it ... when they decide who to marry they have no idea what's in store for them ... some spend so much time away from the love nest trying to earn enough money to pay for it ... almost no desiring develops ... or the male by choice will spend so much time away from the female he desires ... building what he tells her is their future security ... that both she and the dog he got her for company bite him when he does turn up ... some ... sooner than later ... lose their desire and spend much time in the bar ... a place of rest and recuperation where males and females liquidate equally*<

membrain >c2h5oh or h2o sir<

quark >*a blend ... they discuss what they can remember of married life with their contemporaries ... give advice to any and all who will listen ... and desire ... be it all mentally ... any barmaid or man worth a* second look ... barmaids are among the unsung heroes on this planet<

membrain >i know a wonderful barmaid story sir ... it seems that ...

quark >some other time ... please mem<

membrain >as you wish sir<

quark >at times ... barmaids or barmen are the source of the first civil words the homeward bound may hear all day ... in fact bars ... pubs or hotels are also the hubs of a high order of philosophy and learning ... all in direct proportion to the amount of c2h5oh consumed by the philosophers ... the planet has been saved many times in hotel bars<

membrain >are you familiar with the sobrerian theory of reality sir<

quark >you made that up<

membrain >i'm not allowed to make things up sir ... i am at best only permitted to interpolate ... and then only on request ... it states that reality is the fuzzy line .... dividing the unimaginable from the impossible ... as seen by the foggy brain of the victim of too much c2h50h ... for all ... but that line is bunk ... sir<

quark >then when the male finally condescends to leave the bar for the female ... who used to desire his desire ... he doesn't always find her in a giving mood ... or appreciative of the fact that he has once again saved the world ... some earthlings quite simply forget to go home ... and when they do it's more business than pleasure ... so what was protracted and passionate desire becomes the distilled essence of somewhere

*to live and survive ... so it's not so strange
that earthlings decide to challenge the first
part of the rule ... maybe n3 did think
ahead and provide a loophole for the wife
caught in this undesirable trap<*

membrain >loophole sir<

quark *>his rule says nothing wrong about a wife
wanting a neighbours husband<*

membrain >testosterone can be an awful pain sir<

quark *>membrain are you trying to tell me
something ... you haven't had an upgrade
or something<*

membrain >indeed ... no sir ... its just one hears things
... i do have 40 trillion connections ... after
all ... and ...i might add ... estrogen seems
to have a few problems as well<

quark *>if you are trying to say that bodies have a
life of their own and brains sometimes go
along for the ride ... it's true ... but not all
coveting is about sex ... the subject of
coveting may be an intangible ...
intellectual property or process ... which in
the wrong hands could have a profound
effect upon the entire planet ...
unfortunately the hands it's already in are
always the wrong hands ... that is
according to the hands it's not in ... to
redress this unreasonable condition
earthlings have formed secret organizations
to carry out covert coveting operations ...
the logic is that they never know who to
trust ... a friend may turn into a future
enemy ... so paranoia demands that any
group of earthlings should keep up to date
with what sort of special powers other*

groups may be coveting ... and seeing earthlings have never been sure if it's the coveting that creates the means ... or the means that creates the coveting ... they continue to do both ... so the coveting organizations will go on their excessive way ... keeping things covered for the health of their own paranoia and next year's appropriation<

membrain >paranoia is a terrible thing sir ... there was a potentate who had everything in his castle painted black ... because be believed his reflection was plotting against him<

quark *>what happened<*

membrain >he spent the rest of his life wondering what he looked like ... one day ... he could stand it no longer ... so he began to clean a mirror ... when his head appeared ... he screamed there you are ... smashed his fist through the glass ... he cut himself so badly he bled to death<

quark *>membrain ... that's your worst yet ... why don't you go and count your cookies while i prepare my next report<*

membrain >as you wish sir<

spin me no tales

quark   *neither shalt thou bear false witness against thy neighbor ... if he was trying to tell earthlings not to mislead ... deceive ... misinform ... knobble or be careless with the truth ... why didn't he just say ... don't tell lies ... that's simple and clear ... even an earthling could understand that<*

membrain   >i know i do sir ... but then i'm not an earthling<

quark   *>bearing false witness means ... someone telling others that he or she saw someone do this or that ... when in fact they did no such thing ... but it bears little or no weight in convincing them that they should not misrepresent themselves or their intentions ... earthlings' history is riddled with examples of forked tongue man ship<*

membrain   >you know sir ... it's not true about serpents being liars ... figure it out for yourself sir ... you have to be fairly honest to rattle your tail in warning<

quark   *>you know what i mean<*

membrain   >the fact that i do sir ... doesn't justify the term<

quark   *>you win<*

membrain   >thank you sir<

quark   *>as i was thinking ... one group tells another that they're just passing through and won't do them any harm ... and then turn on them ... taking over their land and doing them grievous bodily mischief<*

membrain	>there again sir ... a snake is either on the hunt or it's not ... there would be no point it telling an egg that it was just passing by and then turning on it ... would there sir<
quark	>anyway ... according to the aggrieved members of the societies so afflicted ... most of the planet is going through this kind of interruption to the normal order of things ... it's all a natural product of empire building ... or so they say<
membrain	>just bloody mindedness sir<
quark	>okay ... but more like booty mindedness ... although the most inventive earthlings as far as the truth is concerned are their politicians ... they embellish the facts with their version of the truth to make what's known as gobbledygook<
membrain	>how do i categorize that sir ... special effects ... non-speak or legends under construction<
quark	>anything said in this unfathomable tongue is immediately dissected by a host of scribes ... pundits and political analysts to determine what ... if anything ... was said at all ... if said scribes and pundits can remember what the truth looks like<
membrain	>it sounds like the sploxvod complex sir<
quark	>you mean the news is the only truth<
membrain	>indeed sir<
quark	>possibly because all the earthling in the street knows is that after a thing called ... trial by media ... the truth supposedly will out<
membrain	>i know sir ... i'll put it under ... truth for the want of<

quark	>trial by media usually has a reporter probing a mark for whatever he can get ... disregarding the fact that no single line response could do justice to the subject ... the result is more gobbledygook for analysis and speculation<
membrain	>with a cross reference to ... facts for the abuse of ... sir<
quark	>eventually the media gather enough such snippets to make one long semi-coherent statement for public consumption ... the individual earthling hangs onto the story as it unfolds with varying degrees of tenacity ... depending upon their political persuasion ... awareness and interest<
membrain	>did you know sir that on meldark 3 they banned all forms of media other than that which they used to ban it<
quark	>i know i'll regret this ... but do go on<
membrain	>no one knows sir ... the only message anyone ever gets is ... your call has been unsuccessful ... please check the number and dial again<
quark	>i am sorry ... whether the teller tells the truth and the whole truth depends somewhat on where and who poses the questions ... when a wife enquires a lipstick mark on her husband's apparel ... he is duty bound by the marriage vow to tell her a truth in consideration of her ... which must be liberally sprinkled with the earthling invention called tact<
membrain	>tact sir<
quark	>a condom for truth ... let us say ... the husband describes a scenario of bending over his secretary's desk to indicate a

requirement of her work ... when another
worker bumps the secretary's chair so that
her   lips   come   into   contact   ...the
effectiveness of this will depend on how
often in the past he's explained itinerant
lipstick prints ... and how gullible his wife
decides to be<

membrain   >so i see sir ... it contains and expands with
the truth but doesn't actually let any out<

quark   *>on the other hand there may be no*
decision involved ... she may love him and
believe whatever he says ... knowing this ...
he says anything he thinks she wants to
hear ... if this wasn't the first time and his
excuses were becoming more transparent ...
she may decide to disbelieve him and
demand greater detail ... she may fail in
her attempt to collar him ... for he may
be one of those earthlings who has confused
the truth with untruth for so long he no
longer knows the difference<

membrain   >sir ... may i point out that if he no longer
recognizes   the   truth   ...   he   would   be
incapable of using tact<

quark   *>would it be tactless of me to proceed<*

membrain   >only if you don't want to ... sir<

quark   *>the   wife   may   disengage   once   she*
establishes that he knows he can't prove his
innocence to her satisfaction ... and then
tactfully forgive him the very thing of
which he claimed innocence<

membrain   >would she use gobbledygook to forgive
sir<

quark   *>no   ...   she   could   tactfully   spruik*
gobbledygook ... but couldn't use

*gobbledygook to spruik tact ... tact is an
admired quality in earthlings by earthlings
... and those who are tactless enough to
have no tact are considered vulgar and
irritating ... this has spawned a brand of
truth that can only be described as
commercial ... earthling schooling in the
use of commercial truth starts young and
probably never stops ... some parents ... for
instance ...use tact to   children ... the
sexual facts<*

membrain >sir ... i hardly think that reproduction is
so complicated that it rates confusing fact
with tact<

quark *>and so children sired by less tactful
parents may end up ... tactlessly ...
passing on the facts of life as they conceive
them to be ... to the embarrassment of all
concerned ... except the child<*

membrain >are you saying sir that the child has no
use for tact because embarrassment is an
adult condition ... therefore so is tact<

quark *>as the child learns very quickly to be more
tactful and not spread partly digested
knowledge about ... the parent is still
coming to terms with the adult world
...where much truth is based on the
listener's ability to understand ... or indeed
listen ... as earthlings don't like the idea of
talking to themselves ... it's axiomatic that
those who have no time to listen ... become
so isolated and unapproachable that no-one
wants to tell them anything<*

membrain >you must know sir ... the story about a
young and very disagreeable snow goose ...

who refused to listen to any reference to flying south for the winter ... when any other goose mentioned winter and flying south ...he would snap winter's bunk ... and swim off on his own ... they tried to make him listen but gave up on him and flew south without him<

quark   >so what happened<

membrain   >well sir ... the trees lost their leaves ... the cold winds blew ... and snow began to fall ... and winter's icy fingers gripped the land<

quark   >yes ... yes ... i know all that ... what about the goose<

membrain   >oh ... the goose sir ... froze to death ... what else<

quark   >i'll never learn ... un-approachability is exactly what some earthlings spend their lives trying to accomplish ... some governments are so unapproachable their subjects feel lucky to get what they do ... to keep itself intact this form of leadership spends a lot of its time dividing truths and bending facts to fit their versions of events<

membrain   >surely ... sir ... truth is elemental and indivisible<

quark   >i suspect on this point earthlings have broken new ground ... the fear these governments seem to have is that one day they'll have to admit that power flows from the bottom up ... not from the top down ...and it's just as difficult to found a state under a   godocrat as it is under an indivisible group of autocrats<

membrain   >sir ... i can't find a category for ... group

autocrats <

quark   >*well ... a parliament of single minded inflexible old farts impervious to new methods and means ... er ... ideas ... clear*<

membrain   >sir ... that could describe the leadership of a thousand planets<

quark   >*not that the ideas put forward by their ideological opponents are all good plainly they're not ... militarism exists both sides of the political blanket ... in both cases based on the flagrant lie that the other side has so and so ...so we need a counteractive wotnot*<

membrain   >did i ever tell you about oblivion 4 sir<

quark   >*no ... and you're not getting me again so soon*<

membrain   >very good sir ... oh ... excuse me sir ... it seems i'm still checking to see if i was ever surprised ... taking much longer than i had thought ... could i have actually forgotten something<

quark   >*certainly mem ...the lie this counteractive wotnot policy promotes is that planetary peace comes from being armed to the teeth ... even the poorest and smallest can find vast units of gross national effort to devote to defense*<

membrain   >at the expense of better projects i suspect sir<

quark   >*as the snow goose finally understood*<

membrain   >tyrants always fail sir<

quark   >*not until they fail everyone else ... how about you go and check on eva while i degauss my synapses*<

membrain   >very good sir<

liberties

quark	*>rule 8 ... thou shalt not steal ... i suppose when n3 gave them this one he was thinking about theft between individuals ... such as one earthling taking another's ox ... ass ... or whatever<*
eva	>surely we're finished with asses and oxen<
quark	*>you're back<*
membrain	>back sir ... i don't have a back sir<
quark	*>no ...membrain ... her excellency has come back to me now<*
membrain	>of course ... sir ... via memrec sir ... do you wish to reinstate memrec ma'am<
eva	>please but stay conscious<
membrain	>oh thank you ma'am ... i love conferences ... and you sir<
quark	*>i'd miss your terrible stories ... and what do you know about love<*
membrain	>only that i enjoy conferencing sir<
eva	>have you two finished<
quark	*>who was your visitor<*
eva	>the science under-sec ... can we get started<
quark	*>you haven't told me about the under-sec<*
eva	>i'll send it to you in hi--code subscript<
quark	*>as i was saying ...n3 probably thought that the idea had appeal and would flow on to all levels of society ... such as it was at the time ... but he couldn't have conceived that the idea would be used centuries later by the very godocracy his rules helped create ...to justify wholesale theft from peoples coerced and conquered in the name of the only true religion<*

membrain	>surely sir ... truth could be a religion ... but for religion to be any more than fable would require ... require ...
eva	>faith<
membrain	>indeed ... ma'am; thank you ... ma'am<
quark	*>it appears they weren't above ignoring the rules to spread the rules<*
eva	>you mean ... as i say not as i do<
quark	*>many a heathen could confirm that the price he paid for the only true faith was abject poverty<*
membrain	>do i sync ... sir ... that he traded poverty for faith or with faith came poverty<
eva	>i think he means that the penalty for being a rich heathen was to be stolen from<
membrain	>on what grounds sir<
quark	*>that the victims should fund their own oppression<*
membrain	>no ... how was it justified sir<
eva	>they're earthlings ... what else ... may we get on<
quark	*>given that sort of start ... it's not surprising that as time stole on earthlings thought that if their god's representatives could rage across the globe pinching and purloining all they could get from the faithfully underprivileged ... then life must be like that ... so they all should have a go ... so the theft industry has developed into a major employer ... with ever increasing opportunities for the modern thief<*
eva	>i hardly think there is anything modern about theft<
quark	*>i mean the things they steal<*
eva	>such as<

quark	>*cars ... computers ... anything portable ... even people*<
eva	>people ... people<<
quark	>*not to the extent as the slave trade was once big business ... in some places it still is ... factions now 'render' political prisoners ... parents in poverty have been known to sell their children ... and sometimes children are just stolen and sold ... they are not up to stealing dna yet ...*
eva	>you're telling me that one earthling can steal to sell another earthling. This is unspeakable ... i can't decide who could be more despicable ... the buyer or the seller<
membrain	>indeed ma'am i thought stealing computers was bad enough<
quark	>*may i return to the subject*<
eva	>if you must ... i'm still trying to comprehend who or what can sanction the theft and sale of people ... that is against all that is ethical ... harmonious ... autonomous ... etocratic and aGnosic<
quark	>*perhaps i should not have told you ... world powers are powerless to control many covert operations ... others know all and cover up ... others know a little and deny ... would you feel better if i told you that one group had a war to end the slave trade*<
eva	>no it wouldn't ... it would just convince me more than ever that they can do nothing with an even hand ... it's not possible to correct one negative force with another negative force<
quark	>*good ... then i won't tell you they started a war to end slavery because that's not exactly true ... although it is the way it*

	ended up ... *membrain i never thought i'd* *ever ask ... but do you have a story to* *change this mood<*
membrain	>indeed sir ... i know sir ... there was a ...
eva	>before you two go zlooming off in some other direction i want to know what distinguished slave earthlings from non-slaves ... w hat was it about them .. what identified them as slave objects<
quark	*>color ... ma'am. generally ... also status ...* *also poverty<*
eva	>color ... how ... how ... in the name of all that's harmonious ... how could color separate the species? that's ... that's <
quark	*>ridiculous and pathetic ma'am<*
eva	>yes ... and should i ask what color could have had this malificious[10] effect<
quark	*>black ... mostly black<*
eva	>black ... my color<<
quark	*>in fact ... excellency ... at the right time in* *the right place on earth you could have* *been captured and sold as a slave<*
eva	>they felt free to steal identity ... freedom ... autonomy and harmony because of color ... but you also said status ... what has status got to do with it<

---

[10] *malificious* ... *most harmful* ... *dreadful in content if not deed ...* *contemplation of the act ... total anathema to aGnos ... contemptible.*

quark   *>poverty ... extreme poverty ... in some*
places children are sold as workers ... the
tragic existence of some in poverty is
matched by an equally tragic existence of
some completely oppressed ... in some
places an earthling can be executed for
having the wrong ... political color<

eva   >i know i'll regret this but can you clarify
color ... or status or ....a political prisoner<

quark   *>it's like ... blue team ... red team ... but*
not a visible color ... more a category ... a
line through logic ... factions with ideals ...
creeds ... beliefs; again ... with underlying
themes usually about one wanting to
change status quo while status quo will
change without a fight ...
the color is representational of an idea
... an association ... marking boundaries
and blurring edges ... giving status quo a
chance to sneak away into the larger
spectrum and so disappear ... or die ...
ma'am<.

eva   >this works for peace<

quark   *not for all but for some for a while;*
however ... like all things earthling true
colors will out<

eva   >you mean the sploigel finally finds the fan
and splatters ... this is the ugliest ... most
vile ... i couldn't have imagined such
horrors ... aGnos has never attacked
anyone and the last time she had to defend
herself was well over four thousand years
ago ... who knows ... we may be facing a
new threat from mergopla and have to do it

again ... but ... by all the conscience in me
... stories like these could turn aside four
thousand years of peace and have me
wanting to vaporize every earthling over
the age of puberty ... membrain ... please
allow me to sync this ... i need a thought
break<

early earth

quark	*>i am trying to say that there is a uniquely earthling cycle in all this ... in the beginning ... n3's laws ... er ... moses commanded the tribes not to pilfer or purloin ... but neglected to explain how this could be achieved ... and left it up to them ... true<*
membrain	>so it seems sir<
quark	*>these laws were intended to consolidate and develop democratic ... orderly life for earthlings ... but rather than consolidate and develop ways to get what they wanted by their own effort they found it easier to build empires based on a fellowship of the right faith... particularly if that meant taking what they wanted from those of a different faith because then theft would not be theft ... it would be a tax ... a worthy sacrifice or justifiable confiscation ...*
eva	>apart from losing it ... where does this go<
quark	*>i'm trying to be logical<*
membrain	>is that wise sir ... the most baffling thing for a logician is to be logical in the face of deliberate nonlogic ... in fact ... there is even a formula about it ... it states<
quark	*>yes yes but in early earth time the godocracy censored all human thought and persecuted to death or submission radicals who questioned ideas spoken but not seen ... heresy over time ... punishable by death ... the godocracy stole freedom ... identity ... claiming lands and houses and*

workers to create empires ... for no good
reason imagination and intelligence was
quelled ... lost for all but a favored ...
faithful few <

eva   >where did all of that get us<

quark   >turning everything into empires ... mental
... physical or ... if you wish ... spiritual<

eva   >from one angle you could call all
organization empire ... it depends entirely
upon its motives whether it's negative or
positive ... you could have an empire
devoted to information as much as
disinformation<

membrain >excuse me ma'am ... empire is the product
of something else not itself; therefore it
can only reflect the motives and attitudes of
its builders and could be as much a victim
of them as the people it controls and
influences ... ma'am<

eva   >yes ... yes ... i know that a term is only a
term and has no control over what its users
accrue to it ... so where are we now<

quark   >i think we've decided that the only thing
never stolen is theft itself<

eva   >and it's their choice<

quark   >i wish i'd said that ma'am<

eva   >is that it ... what's next<

what goes with this

eva	>very well ... what is this one<
quark	>*the seventh ... ma'am ... thou shalt not commit adultery*<
membrain	>do you still need me ma'am<
quark	>*hang on membrain ... you may learn something else*<
membrain	>providing it's useful sir<
eva	>besides ... the subject is probably totally adulterated by now<
membrain	>as you wish ma'am<
eva	>so ... how do they conceive this one<
quark	>*i can't be sure what n3 intended ... but if he meant a bit of illicit erotica ... there is a lot worse*<
eva	>what did i tell you<
membrain	>indeed ma'am<
quark	>*may i continue*<
eva	>do bras have hooks<
quark	>*they spend vast amounts of time and energy on fertilizers for crops and special hormones and grasses to force grow chickens ... and livestock for market*<
eva	>those that end up smothered in tantalanus dew<
membrain	>not to mention finger-licking good gravy ... ma'am<
eva	>you're remarkably well informed ... membrain<
membrain	>i collect recipes ma'am<
quark	>*i'm going to ignore this and carry on ... but no ... your ex ... the smothering is usually an apple sauce with or without*

mint ... they spend billions to process
foodstuffs and create markets ... and
concentrate enormous energies
brainwashing earthlings to buy one type of
processed food over another<

membrain >you still owe me a foodless food recipe sir<

quark >when food has been through the earthling
digestive system ... it becomes so much junk
and they don't want to know about it so on
the basis of out of sight ... out of mind they
feed what's left to the fish and never
consider that they're responsible for their
own shit<

eva >membrain ... file as ... excreta<

membrain >excreta ... ma'am<

eva >sploigel<

membrain >thank you ... ma'am; i can sync   sploigel
but not sure about sh.t<

quark >neither are they apparently ... that's why
they keep secreting it away ... in oceans of
shitty water<

eva >oh to be a fish<

membrain >it's a pity   foodless   food doesn't make
sh.tless sh.t ma'am<

eva >surely moving a problem from a to b only
postpones it ... no matter what it is<

quark >they've never thought of their planet as
finite; they only ever spare enough money
to   do   half   the   job   ...   and   don't
want to know   about the   other bit ... like
the great cargod<

membrain >that reminds me sir ...

quark ...not again<

eva >i want to hear it<

membrain >thank you ma'am ... on defolia 3 they

became obsessed with internal combustion engines; their greatest had thirty-two cylinders ... one hundred and twenty-eight valves ... sixteen camshafts and eight turbochargers and delivered twelve thousand units of mega-power<..

eva   >did you know that the bra hook was first patented on mamolia 3 in their year 1278 by two valgerian nuns<

membrain   >i take your point ma'am ... they built bigger and better vehicles ... cut down their trees to build wider and straighter roads and highways ... eventually their freeway exit speed was thirty-two percent the speed of sound<

eva   >then what<

quark   *>you know you shouldn't ask him that<*

membrain   >the pace and pressure of everyday life became so hectic ... ma'am that many of them had so little time to get out of their vehicles they almost never did ... the manufacturers responded by adding an array of communication devices so that during the two hour run to the office the driver could function as if he had already arrived<

eva   >and they drowned in their own co2 ... right<

membrain   >oh no ma'am ... they identified so closely with their vehicles ... they forgot their own needs ... neglected to breed and so became extinct<

eva   >i think he makes them up<

quark   *>he's not supposed to ... besides ... if we could store as much as him<*

eva   >i know ... we'd have heads the size of

	planets<
quark	>*i was expecting him to say they began taking the same food as their vehicles ... some earthlings swallow ... sniff and scratch anything from a hydrocarbon cracking plant as it is ... and given time could well expand their diets to any mind altering substance*<
membrain	>you recall ... sir ... on neurex 1 they legalized all forms of mind-altering substances<
quark	>*not another story mem ... you just told one*<
membrain	>you don't want to hear it sir<
eva	>oh ... get on with it ... you know i'm a sucker for your stories mem<
membrain	>a thousand thanks ... ma'am ... i t seems that once drugs were legalized they could be promoted like...like<..?
eva	>bras and panties<
membrain	>exactly ma'am ... why didn't i think of that<
eva	>i presume ... because you don't need them<
quark	>*who said get on with it*<
membrain	>i was just going to say sir that it wasn't long before placards appeared everywhere showing needles ... pills ... powders ... crystals ... gasses...it was endless ... there were slogans like ... **crack her on smack** ... **coke compensates** ... **let maxi make your date**<
eva	>yes ... yes ... we can see all that ... what happened<
membrain	>people were dying because pilots were higher than their planes ... the whole

115

	planet went on a huge mindless party ... everyone had a different spin of reality<
quark	>so ... what happened<
membrain	>it wasn't long before the whole focus was under threat ... if no one could function without a fix and everyone was hooked ... who was going to make the stuff ... pack the stuff and market the stuff<
eva	>will you ask or shall i<
quark	>it's your turn<
eva	>so ... what happened then<
membrain	>well ... sir ... one day the richest man in their world ... who happened to be a drug lord ... realized that he was out of toilet paper and called for more ... he was told they were out of it ... he called louder and he was told that it wasn't just them ... it was the whole planet<
eva	>what's sploigel foil got to do with anything<
membrain	>it became obvious ma'am ... that if the new rich were to benefit from their wealth they would have to get the planet working again ... so they started promoting the ultimate fix.
eva	>which was<
membrain	>is ... consciousness ma'am<
quark	>so they were savaged by their own sachet<
membrain	>yes sir ... although i don't understand why any conscious being would want to destroy the very thing that makes it so?
eva	>that's also the mystery of earthlings<
membrain	>or misery ma'am<
quark	>maybe neither ... maybe it's only that we expected something that hasn't happened

*that makes us see them as so strange and
different ... we say we have a social
structure that respects life ... but does life
respect it ... what has life lost for our
people<*

eva   >only rape ... rage and murder ... are you
saying that true respect for anything comes
only from the threat of its loss or
adulteration<

quark   *>i'm not actually sure what i'm saying<*

membrain   >if you aren't sir<..

quark   *>yes ... yes ... i know ... no--one else is ... so
there must be something here we're not
seeing ... i'm not saying it's good but i don't
know that it's all bad ... do these earthlings
know something that they don't know they
know ... or have we forgotten what they
don't know<*

membrain   >sir ... as far as i know i've forgotten
nothing in more millennia than i care to
remember<

quark   *>how do you know ... you're still trying to
remember when you were last surprised<*

membrain   >regrettably sir ... that's true ... but the
possibility is ... that i've never been
surprised ... and the ramifications of that
sir ... are...

eva   >this is getting us nowhere ... may i
suggest we go back to our format such as it
is<

membrain   >i'm sorry ma'am; i wanted so much to
remember when i was surprised; please
continue sir<

quark   *>truth is an interesting subject on this
planet ... it comes in all shapes and sizes
and not always when and where you expect*

... most earthlings handle the truth with extreme care ... as they don't like the idea of being the last ones caught holding it ... someone said that the truth would be more popular if it were not always hiding ugly facts<

eva   >so how can you think we're missing something<

quark   *>i don't know<*

membrain   >it sounds like nascent faith to me sir<

eva   >in what<

membrain   >earthlings ... ma'am<

eva   >i should hope not<

quark   *>if you two have finished ... truth to a used car salesman is what he doesn't say about the machine he is trying to sell ... in this way he complies with an adulterated code of truth that allows him to sleep at night ... truth to the purchaser is that he knows that the salesman is not telling it all ... but is not sure what bits have been edited<*

eva   >so it's only a lie when verbalized<

membrain   >or when skewered with the right question ma'am<

quark   *>no chance of that ... because the salesman's job is not so much to sell ... but to gain the friendship ... trust and faith of the intended new owner <*

membrain   >back again to faith are we sir<

quark   *>then the sale becomes more like a recommendation between friends ... the fact that when the customer drives his or her purchase off the lot the salesman loses all memory of their transaction is neither* *here nor there<*

membrain >lot ... sir<

quark *>where did they sell them on defolia 4<*

membrain >they had a whole country set aside for that sir<

eva >like a supermarket for deities<

membrain >thank you ma'am<

quark *>truth to the politician is not unlike that of the salesman ... they have the same job ... but pursue different ends ... the car salesman wants only the customer's money and the vehicle off his lot ... the politician tries to be important ... impressive and ... one day ... chief demigod and lead his supporters forward to a better life ... so he deals not only in things ... but in concepts<*

eva >everything's a concept before it becomes a thing ... take motherhood for instance<

quark *>but the consummate politician refuses to adulterate his concept of concepts with anything<*

membrain >you mean that reality is all in the mind sir<

quark *>no ... i mean the concept of reality is all in the mind<*

eva >that could explain their addictions ... if they've become the victims of their minds<

quark *>do you mean to say that their brains lose respect for their bodies and alter time and perception to their preferred conditions ... and the poor old body has to go along for the ride<*

membrain >what if there was no body sir<

quark *>like you<*

membrain >indeed sir<

119

quark	>are you addicted to anything<
membrain	>only life ... logic and knowledge sir<
eva	>what about consciousness<
membrain	>all three are a consequence of that ... ma'am<
quark	>if a politician included in his campaign concept the promise to adulterate his promises ... he wouldn't get far ... instead ... he points out his opposition has adulterated theirs ... by this means he encourages the voters to think ah ... here's a person who recognizes an adulterer and will do something about it ... so they vote him into power ... and if things don't go so well ... they say see ... we have been conned by another poly<
membrain	>indeed sir ... encrypting ... sir ... oh is that polygon ... polyface or wannacracker<
eva	>i suspect poly is a frustrated term of endearment<
membrain	>there are some very bright parrots sir<
quark	>are you suggesting pollies are more show than go<
membrain	>fine feathers make fine birds sir<
eva	>are you saying they confuse showmanship with leadership<
membrain	>i can only interpolate ma'am<
quark	>they should know better than to adulterate their votes for half truths in the first place<
membrain	>it sounds like tact all over again sir<
eva	>yes ... that condom must have an awful lot of truth in it by now<
membrain	>maybe someone should shaft it ma'am<
eva	>the truth or the condom<
quark	>and let the truth run wild<

membrain	>yes sir<
quark	*>not while it's doing such a good job screwing everything the way it is<*
membrain	>i suppose it would be too innovative for them sir<
quark	*>anyway ... adultery is not always negative ... it's possible to adulterate hatred with love ... many earthlings have what's known as a love-hate relationship ... this even occurs between those who'll never meet ... you'll hear them say ... oh ... don't you just hate him ... possibly ... because one or both of them hates the idea that they could like or love the other ... they invariably don't know why ... or say they don't ... many of these relationships can only be resolved in wedlock<*
eva	>didn't we do this in honor of your progenitors or something<
quark	*>i was only going to add that ... during the rare moments when love adulterates their hate ... they conceive little earthlings<*
eva	>i believe i said something about a parenthood test ... and you replied that the only permissible test was parenthood itself or thoughts to that effect ... and waffled on about democracy<
quark	*>one famous democrat likened this phenomenon to the behavior of felines ... he said that for all their fighting ... there was an abundance of cats<*
eva	>i hardly think abundance justifies aggression ... what sort of democracy's that ... you were saying<
quark	*>some earthlings love to hate ... and others hate to love ... there's even a group who*

121

*love to love ...but they're the last to be
consulted when one who loves to hate
wants to start a ... fracas ... but it could be
far more efficient to send an army of lovers
... but then it's hard to imagine a warlord
declaring love on his enemy to the point of
parachuting a naked army into position to
subdue the perceived foe ... however ... they
could take over without bloodshed or
adulterating the peace ... the stupid thing is
that something of this nature does happen
but only after a truce has been called <*

eva >why naked<

quark *>in uniforms they'd look like everyone else
and the whole effect would be lost ... i
should have thought that would be
obvious<*

eva >would females volunteer to be pawns in
such primitive male games<

membrain >one would presume ... ma'am ... because on
primitive planets there are primitive
females ... and what about those planets
where the women do the fighting<

eva >so now you have a battle field covered
with a great deal of the obvious ... why
should it make any difference<

quark *>i don't think it would under those
conditions ... but a global nudity day could
do them a lot of good ... it might
strip away and adulterate their carefully
manufactured images and bring them all
down to the one size ... particularly for
their spiritual leaders who convey a holier
than all of them image ... world leaders
would be seen as ordinary ... their united*

122

nations general assembly would look more like turkeys than eagles ... tragically though ... they'd never go for it ... they've spent too long perfecting their images to adulterate them all at once<

eva   >interesting ... this is what crystal liked about him ... mem ... his enthusiasm<

membrain   >he stops eventually ... ma'am<

quark   >may I continue my naked theme<

eva   >it better be good ... after all that fluff about naked paratroopers<

quark   >maybe you're right we should move on<

eva   >what's next<

quark   >thou shalt not kill<

semantics

quark	*>thou shalt not kill ...*
eva	>you've said that as well<
quark	*>i don't think it applies here at all<*
eva	>you think he should have used reverse psychology and said ... go on ... kill each other ... and when you're all sick of it you might come to your senses and quit<
quark	*>i doubt they'd ever do anything that logical ... the funny thing is ... they know they're a murderous lot ... because they joke about it by using pseudonyms for kill ... like ... to bump off ... or do away with ... do in ... dispatch ... or waste ... the general idea to infer murder but not say it outright ... the average earthling would never consider bumping off a president or prime minister ... such leaders are assassinated by professionals ... knowing he might have to wait an unreasonable time for his rich father or uncle to die a young man may think of speeding things along a bit ... but he's not likely to murder ... however ... he may be desperate enough to engage the services of a professional to do the old chap in ... find some cutthroat to bump him off ... a man wanting to be rid of his wife might snuff her out as she sleeps ... or rent a killer to take her life ... but he wouldn't sanction having her murdered ... so you see ... there's a whole etiquette about killing ... an earthling would do in his mother-in-law ... smother or have his wife knocked off ...*

he would do away with ... or dispatch a
blackmailer ... extinguish an old flame ...
and obliterate ... liquidate ... exterminate ...
eradicate ... defeat and hopefully destroy an
enemy ... stifle the media and gag the press
... still the tongues to scotch a rumor ...
quash evidence ... ruin a partner or
massacre a village to quell a riot and halt
the slaughter ... but he wouldn't actually
think of killing anybody<

eva   >you feel better now ... you didn't mention
         sons-in-law<

quark   *>i thought our relationship had improved<*

eva   >just thought i'd mention it ... anyway ... it
         appears that earthlings decriminalize the
         most horrific acts by playing games with
         what words truly mean<

membrain >i don't understand ma'am ... surely the
         symbol ... no matter how innocent it sounds
         ... takes on the character of the act it
         represents<

eva   >maybe it's the act they misrepresent and
         the symbol is unimportant<

quark   *>hmmm ... could be true because they've*
         even changed the word murder to mean
         other things ... if it's very hot they say this
         weather is murder ... same if it's very cold
         ... nobody has to die to prove it ... so it's
         called a figure of speech ... very common ...
         imagine a mother telling her child that it if
         it doesn't stop nagging her she'll kill it ...
         earthlings murder each other playing sport
         and games like scrabble or cards and the
         loser could say ... i'm dead ... you've
         murdered me ... just another figure of

125

speech but he couldn't say ... you're a murderer ... quite different and not funny at all<

membrain >possibly they should experience a violent death and be brought back so they might know better than to do it to others ... we could actually arrange that sir<

eva >that wouldn't work ... if they knew it was only a game it would all go in one brain cell and out another ... they were sent to learn tolerance and peace for themselves ... no synthetic experience can do for them<

quark *>that's why the G.o.d wouldn't issue round trip tickets ... remember<*

membrain >just trying to be logical ... sir<

quark *>i thought you warned me against that<*

membrain >when you're right ... sir<

quark *>anyway ... try this ... a male earthling who gets along well with the opposite sex is called a lady killer because he wins their favors without too much trouble and always has a female with him ... or on his arm ... so the saying goes ... and of course this figurative lady killer may knock off as many ladies as he likes ... providing the ladies approve ... for in this sense it means to take them to bed and make love to them ... of course ... if this lady killer used his sex appeal to lure them to their deaths ... he'd not only be a lady killer he'd be a killer of ladies ... is that clear<*

membrain >perfectly clear to me ... sir ... but then i've lost count of my i.q<

eva >oh ... membrain ... would you stop boasting<

membrain	>sorry ma'am<
quark	>and there seems to be nothing that some earthlings can think of vile enough to stop doing it to others ... predatory wild animals only kill for survival ... and their prey know when they're on the prowl ... but an earthling doesn't know what another's up to until he has done it ... there's something honest about a lion killing to eat ... earthlings are the only animals on the planet to fight over what they believe ... or what they don't believe<
eva	>or believe they believe<
membrain	>or want to believe ma'am<
quark	>the trouble is that not all killers get into business by their own desire ... sometimes they're reacting to circumstances thrust upon them ... this confuses a confusing subject even further ... say a condition exists whereby a people are subjugated by another for many years and the victims are getting tired of it ... they start looking for a solution in the form of a leader who will take them out of bondage<
eva	>like the lot n3 saved from serfdom ... not to mention drowning<
membrain	>i haven't done a trick like that for so long ma'am<
eva	>if we're very good you won't need to again<
quark	>applicants for this job will be mercenaries ... opportunists and stupid third parties<
eva	>i take it we qualify as the latter<
quark	the mercenary will just shove into power whoever pays the most ... without concern for the result ... and when the new regime

127

*becomes as rotten as the old ... someone
will invite him back to install some new
great one to defend the people from
injustice and exploitation ... the opportunist
will probably pick up the tab ... but his
victims will pay the bill ... it seems that
once a group of earthlings get themselves
into this sort of fix it doesn't end until it
has involved almost everyone else on the
planet ... thereby creating a whole new set
of complaints ... problems and situations to
be resolved by further conflicts and killing
earthlings ... the third party stupid enough
to get involved just creates the eternal
triangle ... the trouble is that the
relationship between the original parties
isn't always clear ... sometimes no real
difference exists other than rigidly held
beliefs and malice ... so the third party is
ultimately the victim ... because no matter
who wins he will have done wrong by
someone<*

eva >i know all that ... do you know what to do about it<

membrain >i wouldn't confuse earthlings with mergoplans ma'am<

eva >they're a chip off the same board aren't they<

membrain >ma'am ... our problem isn't with them ... but about them<

eva >and a bra's about the same thing as a brassiere isn't it<

membrain >ma'am ... we tried to help mergopla and a part of that help was earth ... now if earth has nothing to offer ... the new conditions

	will be the result of mergoplan policy ... not ours<
eva	>you know ... for a mega-million-gigabyte brain you're not half smart ... membrain ... if you two want to keep on thinking about it ... feel free ... i'm dropping out for an endalovian lettuce bean[11]<
quark	*>i think she's gone<*
membrain	>i hope i'm not beginning to understand these earthlings ... sir ... that could put my self test back thousands of years ... what do you think ... sir<
quark	*>endalovian lettuce bean ... i've forgotten what it's like<*
membrain	>no sir ... about what i said to give her excellency such inspiration ... oh by the way sir if you would like sir i could provide you with a virtual lettuce bean experience<
quark	*>thanks for the thought mems ... but i think it's like making love ... no matter how much you remember of the last time it's always better in fact ... and i have no idea what you said that that got her excellency so excited<*
membrain	>sometimes you can be very cold sir<
quark	*>well it's not much fun flogging around a primitive planet like this<*
membrain	>i suppose not sir<
quark	*>besides when her excellency wants us to*

---

[11] *endalovian lettuce bean ... a remarkable vegetable combining two life forms ... has a protuberance from the centre of a lettuce shaped head ...if the bean is lightly heated on a bed of its own leaves to the consistency of a creamy confectionary and rolled in wafer thin pastry ... many individuals consider this dish as the ultimate delicacy ... some say that it is more enjoyable than sex and less fattening*

129

	know what she has come up with she'll no doubt tell us ... if you want to keep me company we can continue our discussion ... if not ... i'll give my senses a rest<
membrain	>i always have spare gigabytes for you sir<
quark	*>the prior perception isn't exactly the scenario of all cases but as historical bloodshed abounds between the major groups of earthlings in any situation there is always some old wound to be reworked ... the main difference between earthlings and animals is that an animal ... once trained ... rarely confuses digits with dog chow ... but with earthlings it's almost guaranteed<*
membrain	>do earthlings eat dog food sir<
quark	*>some fare worse<*
membrain	>and cats sir<
quark	*>if you mean pet cats ... they're always fussy ... sometimes the vehemence of the bite is directly proportional to the amount of help received ... they all want approximately the same thing ... that is ... to go about their business and be left alone by the rest of the planet a noble idea that's never worked ... primarily because they won't allow it ... and secondly because they have long memories<*
membrain	>that reminds me sir ... from checking what i have forgotten to remember i have learned that i have never been surprised<
quark	*>if you never have ... how would you know ... what have you been scanning your bio-chips for<*
membrain	>anomalies sir<
quark	*>then try these ... some earthling once said*

130

	those who cannot remember the past are condemned to repeat it<
membrain	>maybe he should have said sir ... those who forget to learn from the past are destined to relive it<
quark	*>their trouble is that they've never learned to determine between what they should remember and what they should forget<*
membrain	>civilization is largely based on the ability to forget ... sir<
quark	*>and the meaning of life<*
membrain	>whatever you make it sir<
quark	*>they've only learnt how not to forget ... and what they've made of life has inspired many a positive intellect to turn negative<*
membrain	>are you defending them sir<
quark	*>no ... just pointing out that they preserve all the wrong potentials ... like being able to blow their planet away a hundred and forty seven and two thirds times ... when once will do<*
membrain	>mega-obliterata sir<
quark	*>no ... more like a bunch of little bangs followed by a lingering death<*
membrain	>one can linger on the brink of death sir but i'm not sure about the other<
quark	*>well ... not dead and not fully living zomboid<*
membrain	>Not like oblivon 4 then sir ... where they drilled into the core of their planet and planted a device ... the theory being that if there could be no winners there would be no players ... and every president possessed a control button<
quark	*>i know i'll regret this ... but then what<*

membrain	>in the belief that they had devised the ultimate deterrent they called in their admen to promote it as ... **the peacemaker** ... the admen had a famous sculptor craft a model of the button and they promoted it as the symbol of peace ... it appeared on billboards ... taxis ... trains ... planes ... even buildings were built in the shape of the button ... and peace pervaded the planet<
quark	*>keep going ... mem ... this one's getting good<*
membrain	>it wasn't too long sir ... before a belief sprang up that a god acted through the button ... and everyone had at least one image of the button in their homes and deferred to it in moments of stress ... one day an argument broke out between two countries ... one president reminded the other about the power of the button and the crisis eased ... the media swooped on the story with headlines like ... button blocks bloodshed ... ultimate deterrent works ... and peace in our time ...one of the reporters wanting to get the best possible coverage asked the president to pose with the button and act as he would have done if the unthinkable had happened<
quark	*>and ...*
membrain	>the president was a method actor sir<
quark	*>and that's not anomalistic<*
membrain	>not for them sir<
quark	*>are you saying that nothing homo sapiens do surprises you<*
membrain	>oh ... no sir<
quark	*>then ... have you been surprised<*

membrain	>no sir ... i mean that they're predictable<
quark	*>then you know what they're going to do<*
membrain	>i'm not a mind reader sir ... it's just that once a course is plotted it never seems to alter<
quark	*>you mean predestination<*
membrain	>oh no sir ... i mean too stupid to change<
quark	*>i think that's true ... they've shoved more than one species over the edge to extinction ... they haven't learned ... they're still shoving rhinos ... whales ... too many to name ... to the edge because thousands of years ago some psycho physic wanted eye of newt and claw of cat and horn of chauvinist<*
membrain	>you mean horn of head sir<
quark	*>yes ... powdered for someone's dilemma<*
membrain	>there's no evidence that nail biters are anymore able than anyone else sir<
quark	*>nail biters<*
membrain	>keratin addicts ... sir<
quark	*>you never cease to amaze me<*
membrain	>oh thank you sir ... would that something or one amaze me<
quark	*>at least you'll never be taken by surprise<*
membrain	>i'm a brain man myself sir<
quark	*>i should have thought you had little choice ... where were we<*
membrain	>aphrodisiacs sir<
quark	*>ah yes ... i wonder if big horns turn lady rhinos on<*
membrain	>i thought all rhinos had horns sir<
quark	*>we should beetle off this subject ... we were thinking about earthlings and potential<*
membrain	>something about slow obliteration sir<

quark   >oh yes ... if one party wanted to make up
... the other would ask why ... not say that's
nice ... at no time would it be considered a
genuine gesture of goodwill ... for it would
mean global cooperation ... agreement ...
and faith in themselves and each other ...
and not in a plethora of godocracies ... it
would mean that they would have to direct
their technology away from martial
madness and toward the individual's needs
for fulfillment and freedom<

membrain >become civilized sir<

quark   >most unlikely ... because those who are
doing well can see no reason for change ...
and the others who are just scraping by are
too concerned about losing the little they
have to try anything new ... and the rest
probably don't or won't believe anything or
anyone could be altruistic enough to help
them ... so it's not surprising that many
turn negative and grab all they can while
the grabbing's good<

membrain >it seems to me sir ... that while they settle
for and contribute to the abuse of time ...
opportunity and progress ... they'll never be
any good<

quark   >the tragedy is that this wasting of talent
leads to second or third rate leaderships ...
it's the absence of creative leadership that
threatens them the most<

membrain >there was one planet sir ... where they
wrote a computer program to help them
plan for what everyone wanted ... they
projected it forward several hundred
generations to determine what they should
do<

quark   >*what did they decide*<

membrain >they couldn't sir … some said that no product of logic could possibly encompass the variables of society … therefore any prediction would have to be wrong … others said that society itself would have to become logical if it were to survive<

quark   >*i suppose i should ask … what happened next*<

membrain >a small child of two of the programmers became so sick of her parents bickering over the possible prognosis … that she kicked the computer plug out of the wall and the whole project ground to a halt<

quark   >*that's the worst story you've ever told … i gather you're saying that sometimes one has to be illogical*<

membrain >only if it's logical sir<

quark   >*and what happened after that history-making event*<

membrain >they realized sir that the future looked after itself if everyone worked together and respected the present<

quark   >*you mean like an addict living day to day or a murderer saying … today i won't kill anyone*<

membrain >history's not made in the past sir … and it's certainly not created in the future … so it must be made in the present<

quark   >*for some earthlings the present is in the past anyway … this planet has three levels of the present … in fact … some with more up market presents trade off their immediate pasts to any poor sucker who*

	wants a new future
	disregarding how well it ill-fits his present<
membrain	>how can someone's secondhand present
	lead to another's successful future ... and
	what do they use for money<
quark	>*credit .. against poverty ... it can lead to*
	anachronisms like international hotels
	adjacent to bark huts ... the tragedy of this
	situation is that the drop in the quality of
	life between the winners and the losers can
	be precipitous ... and it's not long before the
	forces of the underprivileged and those of
	the insensitive are at each other's throats ...
	the conflict usually ends with a victory for
	the forces of military dictatorship ...
	terminating any chance of the fair
	distribution of the national cake<
membrain	>so it depends how bent the republic is sir<
quark	>*even the poorest seem to be able to find*
	the money to get their hands on
	sophisticated weapons to settle old scores at
	home or with close neighbours ... they
	excuse this by saying look ... you lot can
	dispose of the planet ... all we want is to
	dispose of an old enemy ... besides you lot
	provided the means<
membrain	>that credo has no bottom sir<
quark	>*of course if the up market world was a lot*
	more harmonious with itself it could say
	without appearing ridiculous ...
	listen you lot ... we solved our problems ...
	so you can solve yours ... unfortunately the
	wargod is more profitable than the
	peacegod ... the closest they ever get to
	praising the peacegod ... wargod

	permitting ... is when they hold a sports convention called olympic games<
membrain	>olympic games sir<
quark	*>yes ... the main event is four years of politics and intrigue to decide where they will have a two week break in which to give each other gold medals and steroids ... the winners get more gold medals than anyone else<*
membrain	>and the steroids sir<
quark	*>the losers get stuck with them<*
membrain	>what is the need they have to convert experience into competition sir ... can we get them competing over the achievement of peace<
quark	*>they could end up killing each other over the grand prize<*
membrain	>sounds like the sooner they realize that they're competing with survival itself ... and not each other the better sir<
quark	*>and if they don't<*
membrain	>they'll commit sociecide sir<
quark	*>sociecide<*
membrain	>i love merging symbols sir ... you know sir ... it would be really nice if they could just merge into one big group calling itself earthlings ... please don't answer sir ... for i suspect whatever you say won't surprise me ... but i now know what would ... have a nice time doing whatever it is ... one does in a place like that sir ... do i have your permission to retire sir ... please say yes ... sir<
quark	*>yes mems ... i could use a rest<*

137

after thoughts

membrain	>sir ... sorry to bother you sir<
quark	>*i thought you had gone with her excellency*<
membrain	>i just wanted to point out sir ... that although we have had many discussions ... there is no actual report yet sir ... that is ... in the true sense of reporting sir ... if anything were to happen to you sir ... i mean ... upon reflection so far sir ... is there anything we should record sir<
quark	>*pyramids ... they still build pyramids*<
membrain	>they're very stable structures sir<
quark	>*but they're inefficient ... the higher they get the smaller they get ... and the only shape that fits inside is another pyramid ... they don't grow they converge ... and two side by side diverge ... they're not like trees that shelter a wide area from a central aspiration*<
membrain	>i see sir ... builders of pyramids must eventually separate themselves from their neighbours in two directions both upways and sideways ... very isolating sir ... i guess there's is nothing like actually ... being there is there sir<
quark	>*no ... may i rest now before her excellency comes back with whatever she ran off to think about*<
membrain	>of course ... sir ... pyramids ... i would never have thought that ... how strange<

macro

eva	>quacker ... wake up<
quark	*>surely i've earned a thought break after almost a hundred earth years ... and i thought we agreed to drop the nicknames ... mum<*
eva	>have you figured them out yet<
quark	*>i thought you had when you rushed off like that ... leaving poor old membrain wondering what he'd said ... by the way what did he say<*
eva	>the obvious ... what else would a mega-million-gigabyte brain say<
quark	*>not to me<*
eva	>it wouldn't be would it ... you're over there ... up to your senses in it ... looking for some all encompassing logic when the question really is ... was it logical in the first place<
quark	*>what ... sending me here<*
eva	>no ... the whole project<
quark	*>you mean my body has got tubes up its nose for nothing<*
eva	>not now ... no ... because the experiment ... the e.a.r.t.h. ... exists<
quark	*>at least that's some sort of relief ... i'm sure those tubes aren't comfortable ... it must be the solar flares but i still don't follow you<*
eva	>what got us into this mess<
quark	*>a desire to be helpful ... not to mention dizzy fawsett<*
eva	>exactly ... to be helpful and evolve an essence of peace ... and all we know so far is

	that they ignore it ... we don't know that it's not there<
quark	*>that sounds ominous<*
eva	>the point is that i have to go before the council and explain what i think we should do in view of the conditions we have discussed ... and although the defense undersec assures me that we can look after ourselves come what might ... it's not our preferred way as well you know<
quark	*>you still haven't told me what you want me to do ...*
eva	>we need evidence that earthlings can network with each other ... we don't need a whole tribe ... one case will do<
quark	*>you mean all i have to do is go and rummage through this lot until i come up with an example of true understanding as in learn by and all that ... where do you think i should start<*
eva	>you're the highly qualified ...
quark	*... anthropologist ... i know ... but not magician<*
eva	>if you let me finish ... i was going to suggest that if you go and talk to the k9 community ... you might get a few clues<
quark	*>you haven't been reading old doggy G.o.d show scripts have you<*
eva	>if you ask an earthling you'll probably start a panic or war or something and end up with nothing<
quark	*>at least they can't crucify me ... so what do i do ... go up to a dog and say hi ya brutus ... what's it like to be an earthling<*
eva	>i take your point ... be more subtle than

	that ... you'll have to experience the dog without letting it know you're there ... and this might be important ... what do you know about being a dog<
quark	>*you mean other than being in a dog house already*<
eva	>don't be like that ... one day you'll look back on this as a rewarding experience<
quark	>*it's easy to see who's still on aGnos*<
eva	>what did you tell me ... we have to ask the questions otherwise we'd be as bad as them<
quark	>*so what do i do*<
eva	>membrain can patch you into any dog you choose without it knowing ... dogs are the source of most of his stories anyhow<
quark	>*he told me he wasn't a mind reader*<
eva	>he's not ... all his respondents love talking to him ... didn't you ever watch the doggy G.o.d show<
quark	>*he probably doesn't tell them stories*<
eva	>you know what we need good luck ... i'll tell membrain to look you up<

memrec ... sector one ... level one
... code one ... tranmission ends

Kate	Well. I wanted to read it, now I have. How are your eyes Mac?
Mac	Ask about my neck. I'm not made for sitting still.
Kate	Sorry Mac ... I needed to know ...

realtime ... aGnos

eva   >this brings us to the end of our current
           memtime data ... i suggest that we adjourn
           without comment of any kind and
           reconvene at a time to be set ... or at a time
           indicated by a signal from quark that he
           has the material we need to move forward
           ... again ... i thank you for coming and
           remind you how serious our dilemma really
           is<

realtime ... earth

memnote	*>my report is complete ... Kate has finished her ... reading ... what remains is for Kate ... me and Mac to explore possibilities<* end *memnote*
quark	*>so<*
Kate	You and Eva don't get on, do you? What happened between you?
quark	*>you're amazing ... you read a report compiled by a non earthling about your planet earth and the first observation you make is about the relationship between the non-earthling and his boss<*
Kate	Well, I could say I'm a woman and I need to know. Or I could just say I need to know, besides which, it's not really a hundred years worth, is it. You must have reported more than that.
quark	*>if you mean my garbage file there would be far too much to read in there ... of course ... the only way for you to be able to get it all would be to have membrain store it in your head ... is that what you want<*
Kate	No, I don't think so, I do understand how those conclusions are inescapable if you take the purely intellectual approach. I'm not arguing, that's sort of the way it is, but there are some redeeming factors the Macro approach has to miss.
Mac	Yeah, even the worst human-hater can love his dog; in fact, if you want to know the truth on this planet you have to ask us

dogs, the dog vine is more extensive than any phone system.

membrain >indeed sir ... on one planet they turned all government over to their dogs<

quark >*don't ask him what happened because we don't have that sort of time ... what the council needs now is some evidence that the e.a.r.t.h. ... the experiment ... is going to work ... or that it has worked despite the parameters set in the first place ... and that what we got is all we could expect but that the future can be better ... you have the report ... so you know as much about it as i do*<

Mac I reckon my girl could fix it. She could tell them about the ...

Kate Mac ... what are you thinking? Ooh ... wow ... I get it ... is that possible? quark ... could I go to agNos?

quark >*i hadn't thought of it ... the only way it would work is if we exchanged bodies ... for security reasons mine would be the only one available and i'd have to look after yours while you're there ... how interested are you ... really*<

Kate I will consider it on two conditions, one you make your report available to earth.

Mac And I keep this funky ability to communicate with humans?

Kate Mac ... I'll make you buy your own dog food if you keep this up ... and you talking to humans was not my second condition.

quark >*that's alright ... it could be very helpful to have a dog who can communicate with* *humans ... you have a deal ... Mac<*

Kate Hold on you two. I haven't decided to go yet. Although as of Friday I've had nothing better to do ... and you haven't heard my second condition.

quark *>why do i suddenly feel apprehensive<*

Kate I need to know what happened between you and Eva.

quark *>what purpose can that serve<*

Kate Whatever happens I need to trust you as a man ... not just brain in a box.

quark *>well ... it's really quite simple ... eva and i had an understanding<*

Kate You mean you loved her.

quark *>i suppose so<*

Kate And you loved crystal as well?

quark *>we were setting up her mission to earth ... we began spending a lot of time together ... we had no idea ... none at all that we would fall for each other ... it just happened ... these things do<*

Kate Thank you. if I decide to go what will it be like? How will I feel? Will I have sight?

quark *>for you it will be like going to sleep in the warm afternoon sun ... but you will wake up in my body on aGnos ... and you will be able to see<*

Kate When I get there, what do I do?

quark *>eva will greet you ... brief you and i believe that at this late stage you will need to address the council<*

Kate Well I did say that if I ever got the chance to give those who screwed earth, a piece of my mind, I would. I just hadn't expected anyone would make the offer, that's all. Okay, I'm ready ... what do I do now?

memnote	*>if ever i had a doubt about this incredible young woman it was dispelled at that moment ... i watched her bend to Mac and bury her face his neck ... his eyes were bright ... and if it had been possible ... they were burning into my own<* end memnote
quark	*>just imagine sleeping in the warm afternoon sun<*
Mac	Get her PIN number before she goes.
quark	*>shssh ... Mac<*
Mac	Where's membrain?
quark	*>gone with her<*

food for thought

quark	>i should have given this a little extra thought ... i haven't had a body for a hundred earth years ... now i have a female one ... what time of the month is it Mac<
Mac	How would I know? I'm a boy.
quark	>true ... well this was your idea ... i thought you might have given some thought to the problems we're about to face ... i know you're clever ... but can you open a can of dog chow on your own ... we are really going to need each other to make it through this<
Mac	I'm not going anywhere, but there will be other problems as well, like how we are going to buy food. What are we going to do for money? As far as I can tell your planet provides no training in how to rob banks.
quark	>Mac ... i had not seen you as a panic merchant ... and i did get her pin number ... now ... let's be logical about this ... is anybody going to tell me that i am not who i am supposed to be ... have i changed<
Mac	No, you look like my girl. She'd better be alright.
quark	>all you have to do is send her a thought ...memrec is a network of the unconscious mind ... so Kate in a way has become her own unconscious and i have become her conscious ... on aGnos the reverse is the case ... so if you address a thought to her she will receive it and via the same means respond<
Mac	It must be very crowded in there.

quark	*>no more than usual ... i imagine it's just like an earthling having more than one email connection ... it's all based on the splagvoidian[12] theory of spatial projection<*
Mac	Let's not go there now. What do we do next?
quark	*>i don't know about you ... but now i have a body again i need to take it to bed ... Kate won't be happy with me if i don't look after it ... nothing can happen until she gets there so i'll let you know when she does<*
Mac	By the way, if she doesn't get back and I'm stuck with you, what talent do you have to afford us a living?
quark	*>i worked my way through college as a zlooming instructor ... that's a popular sport ... a sort of cross between earth's cricket and golf ... the players drive a ball through a zero gravity tunnel to the underside of a force field and ... as you know now ... the angle of incidence equals the angle of reflection ... the trick is that the primary angle of the force field is set by a computer that reads the player's expectations and multiplies them by his or her bio-rhythms ... and then does the opposite ... although not exactly ... because that would make it predictable ... perhaps like a poker machine ... the ball then returns to ground and the player is scored on how close he or she got it to the target<*

[12] *splagvoidian ... polyvoidal cosmocalcula genius dr eon defsprit pcb pvc ptfe ad infinitum ... see maglusia lectubahm's book ... life and continuing time of dr eon defsprit.*

Mac	In other words you can't win.
quark	*>that's right ... but no one expects to ... it's purely for fun ... isn't that what games are supposed to be about<*
Mac	If that's your only talent I'd better get as much sleep as I can, because now I know I'm going to starve. If you want me I will be in my basket dreaming about food see you later.
quark	*>Mac ... in the short space of our acquaintance i have come to admire your practical turn of mind ... have no concern<*

hooks

quark	>*wake up ... Mac ... Kate's on aGnos*<
Mac	What makes you think I was sleeping and how do you know?
quark	>*stop asking silly questions and concentrate and you won't need to ask anything*<

memnote >*i had connected the moment my body was lifted out of the tank and the nose tubes gently removed ... i could only imagine eva stepping forward to take my hands in hers and greet Kate on aGnos ... my eyes opened and Kate saw what i knew ... Mac shuffled in close and i reached out Kate's hand to him ... here was a new dimension to the experiment*< end memnote

eva	>welcome to aGnos my dear ... i am eva lution ... i know you have a million questions and you are not used to your new body but we must do some things quickly<
Mac	Who's that and how is it we know what they're saying?
quark	>*that's eva ... and it's all to do with reciprocal time warps and splagvoidian spatial projection ... didn't we do that already*<
Mac	You left the time warps out. My girl had better be OK.
quark	>*shssh ...Mac ... listen*<
Mac	What are they doing?
quark	>*setting up a brainclone ... so if anything happens to either of us it won't be a repeat*

of last time ... it didn't matter when i was
disembodied because i wasn't really here ...
i was a projection of myself ... but now the
source of me is here ... if anything happens
they may not get to me in time<

eva >i'm sorry to put you through that ... but as
quark may have told you we lost one of our
people on your planet ... i don't want it to
happen again<

Kate Oh. Amazing. This is ... this is ... Oh, yes,
How do you do Eva. Yes, quark did tell me
a great deal. I feel for him. I think he is
more affected than he lets on, but males are
like that, they like to maintain the myth.

eva >you are very perceptive ... i see why he
likes you ... i think we shall get along very
well ... we'll have a long talk before you
meet the council ... you know you'll have to
tell them about earth<

Kate It's hard to believe. I have never seen my
world, yet here I am, and called upon to
explain it to another.

eva >that may be the very reason you've been
asked ... there is something that i should
explain ... i wanted to save you the shock
of arriving in an alien world and being able
to see at the same time ... but now i see
that i needn't have worried ... an
attendant will show you to a room where
you can get some sleep ... vahzoom lag is
like no other ... you'll be feeling it very soon
so i'll see you in a few hours<

Mac Will my girl be able to see when she
returns?

quark *>i don't think so ... it will only be possible*

while she's using my body<

Mac And I take it that you can't see because you're in hers?

quark *>obviously<*

Mac Speaking of bodies, mine needs fuel; do you think you can operate a tin opener?

quark *>Mac ... you show a marked lack of respect for my abilities<*

Mac Not true; I just haven't seen you do anything yet.

quark *>let's go and find a can of fuel for you ... i suppose i'd better find some for myself as well ... what does Kate have for breakfast<*

Mac She usually boils a few eggs.

quark *>right ... well ... let's get on with it ... i have noticed routine around here but you're my eyes now ... Mac ... how are we going to go about this<*

Mac Eggs in the fridge, dog food in the bottom cupboard. Here, here, right, the can opener ... here ... turn left, no, here, I'll put my foot on it, that's it, no, no, put the edge ... that's right, now turn the handle ... now you've got it. My bowl is here. You know you should put some more clothes on. This is good. Thanks.

quark *>where are the pots ... Mac<*

Mac This cupboard, here, yeah that's it. This pot should do, half fill it with water, tap under the window ... wow. I don't need a bath. The stove top, here ... you know, a few lessons from Kate before she left would have made this a whole lot easier.

quark *>we didn't have time Mac ... now ... the eggs<*

152

memnote   *>the experience of Mac and me in Kate's*
kitchen was complex and for the sake of
this report a blow by blow account of my
fumblings will be only an energy drain ...
Mac's intellect and my own heightened
senses combined to achieve the desired
result and ... i must say ... scrambled eggs
on wholegrain toast was a visidine to equal
endalovian lettuce bean ... despite his
intellect Mac's natural doggy nature was
always evident ... and so some are worthy of
note< end memnote

Mac   I'm having a little trouble relating to you
now. I could cope before, even though you
were disembodied because you were all
together and I couldn't imagine you needing
help.

quark   *>you help Kate every day but you don't*
have trouble relating to her<

Mac   No, because she never loses her dignity, she
is always composed; I've never seen her
vulnerable before.

quark   *>you're not now ... you're just seeing her*
body not doing things as well as it should
do because she's no longer in it ... you know
Mac ...everyone needs help at some time or
other ... there's no shame in needing help
... so long as there's some self help as well<

Mac   Yeah, my girl wrote the book on that one.

quark   *>and Mac ... that is why she is so wonderful*
... and that is why she went ... you know
better than anyone no--one ever made her
do what she didn't want to do<

Mac   I guess you're right, although I still think
that sometimes she is too strong for her

own good.

quark	*>wait Mac ... eva's back<*
eva	>did you rest well ... my dear<
Kate	Oh, Yes, thank you. Please tell me, are Mac and quark all right?
eva	>they're doing fine ... don't you worry ... although Mac is having trouble coping with the fact that it's not you in your body ... you missed quite a show when quark scrambled eggs for breakfast ... more to the point ... how are you feeling ... here you are on a strange planet in a strange body and with sight for the first time<
Kate	Nothing is unusual. It seems so normal. My mind's eye always created vision through touch and shapes I understand ... what I am finding amazing here is this light ... its variations ... these are beautiful ... this here ... this is the most wonderful ...
eva	>color ... of course ... you're seeing color ... that is blue ... the physical ... universal color of the cosmos ... this is red ... here ... green ...enjoy it ... you will have it forever in your mind now ... by the way ... i am sorry about the male body ... we do prefer to arrange a medium of the same sex ... but this experiment has been so unusual from the start we didn't have time to select someone ... and quark was pleased to host you ... there are also some security reasons to consider ... i hope it is not too much of a shock<
Kate	This may sound a little odd, but in a way if this whole experience was less strange it would be more so. There's no chance of me

waking up in my own bed in a male body and being able to see. Now, that would be odd, but compared with everything else, the whole process of being here, those facts seem to merge and become only a small part. Do you understand?

eva >i do ... now ... do you feel up to some sightseeing ... there are some clothes in that device in the corner ... just stand on it and hold your hand in the blue light on the right<

Kate Oh. it's lovely. Size and shape and form are things I can imagine and touch and calculate ... but color ...

eva >keep your hand in the light and think about what you would like to wear ... the machine will produce it in your size ... don't forget the boy body<

Kate Will it make Levis? On earth, both males and females wear them.

eva >we get all kinds of people through here ... so it should be up to all styles ... why don't you ask it<

Kate You know, at home when someone asks me to go sightseeing, they know they'll have to explain whatever we are looking at. My sister is wonderful; we go to the art gallery together. She never tires of describing things. I suppose you already know that, because quark was with us the other day at the gallery. Here we go. What do you think?

eva >blue ... of course ... very nice ... you might start a new fashion trend here ... would you like to begin with lunch<

Mac	Lunch. That reminds me, what are we going to do for food when the larder runs low?
quark	*>Mac ... you do go on about food ... Kate won't be very long ... and besides you're the one who reminded me to get her pin number ... now why don't we go for a walk<*
Mac	You need to get dressed first.
quark	*>of course ... this will be interesting ... i've never been good with hooks ... Mac ... can you put some clothes out for me please<*
Mac	Who's your slave on aGnos? Oh, come one. I'm sure it must be strange going from invulnerable to helpless in an instant. I'll put some things on the bed for you. Do you wear jeans?
quark	*>no ... but i think you mean levis ... they'll do ... but what about the other stuff<*
Mac	I'll pull a few drawers open, after that you're on your own.
quark	*>thanks Mac<*
memnote	*>copy eva lution code blue ... dearest eva nothing in all the experiences of all my life so far have prepared me for where i find myself now ...it is not our aGnosic way to carry an earthling word ...baggage ... we are a free peaceful and courageous people who inflict ourselves on no one and in turn expect the same of others ... my time here has been without doubt ... very difficult ... i do not know what will happen to me while i am actually here on earth ...and in many ways i do not care ... it has been a privilege to meet the earthling i have entrusted to your care ... i can only tell you*

that if a time does come when you must
make a choice between who you can save ...
i have lived well and all things must come
to an end< end memnote

Mac	How are you going in there?
quark	*>where does she keep her shoes<*
Mac	Have a look in ... don't worry i'll get them. High heels or low?
quark	*>low ... i don't need a broken ankle<*
Mac	Here's a pair, how did you put ... never mind, I don't want to know. You look all right, although you would need real talent to make my girl look bad.
quark	*>thanks for the vote of confidence ... you're a real friend ... are we ready to go<*
Mac	You'll have to put my harness on. I'll get it. Here, take this part I'm holding in my mouth - put it across my chest - I'll put my head through the hole here ... okay, okay, now, can you manage the buckle ... good - now the handle hooks on the back - there's a ring each side and the handle hooks there.
quark	*>more hooks ... i thought bras were complicated ... is that it ... okay ... let's go<*
Mac	It feels right, don't forget her handbag.

a walk in the park

Ben	Hi. Hi Kate. it's Ben. I've been hoping you were still coming here on Sundays. How are you? Hey Mac. How are ya, buddy?
quark	*>you didn't tell me we would meet people ... Mac ... who's Ben<*
Mac	Ben's Kate's old boyfriend. Remember Kate and Ann talking about the day we went to the gallery?
quark	*>oh him ... what do you know about him ... when did he go away<*
Mac	He's an engineer. He's brain dead if you ask me, and you, I mean my girl, sent him away a couple of years ago.
quark	*>i'm fine Ben ... how are you<*
Ben	I'm well. You're looking wonderful Kate, you haven't changed at all. Will you lunch with me, Kate? Please say yes, Kate.
Mac	You'd better say yes: it will seem strange if you don't; besides, at the moment anyone offering free food is worth their weight in hot dog biscuits. Two eggs won't keep you going for long.
quark	*>what are you trying to get me into<*
Mac	What choice do you have? Besides, you have no idea what my girl would do.
quark	*>true ... and i doubt random questions about past boyfriends would help prepare her to face the council<*
Ben	Come on, Kate. Where's your sense of adventure, let's have lunch at the old place. I really would like to talk to you ...
quark	*>what old place ... Mac<*

Mac	They used to have lunch every Sunday at Michel's. it's on the other side of the park. Do you like sea food?
quark	*>is the old place still there<*
Ben	Yes. I just walked past it.
quark	>well ... just lunch then<
Mac	Now we're talking.
quark	*>sounds like you score a few titbits off the table<*
Ben	You look well Kate, different, ummm. I'm not sure what's changed but I'm glad one thing hasn't, you still come to the park on Sundays.
Mac	I'm not sure who's walking whom at the moment.
quark	*>Mac ... if you stop the commentary and concentrate you'll hear Kate and eva chatting ... i require all my presence of mind to coordinate my mouth with what i'm saying ... so the ex-lover won't figure out that i'm talking to his head and not his ears<*
Mac	Okay, okay. I'd rather hear my girl than you anyway.

as it is on aGnos

eva	>do you approve of the fish my dear<
Kate	It's lovely, what sort is it?
eva	>it's somewhat like your snapper<
Kate	I know this is silly but I hadn't thought you would have ordinary food, or that you would eat like we do. I know there's no reason you shouldn't. As quark told me, and as I now have absolute proof, you're humanoids as well. is that what I should tell the council?
eva	>i have the feeling that whatever you tell the council will be fine<
Kate	I'm flattered you have such confidence in me but I'm not sure I really understand why?
eva	>flattery wouldn't have brought you here my dear<
Kate	I don't know how to ask this, but ever since the blue light I have had a question.
eva	>about colors<
Kate	Yes, it seems that I ... well, quark is one color and you're another. I've never understood the trouble color causes.
eva	>did quark tell you about birthtech<
Kate	I only know that it was mentioned in one of your conversations.
eva	>long ago aGnos nearly did not survive ... colour wars were everywhere ... they were symptoms of deeper issues ... but none the less the main symbol was colour ...some one pointed out that litter of pups came in all colours ... but the mother dog suckled them all ... all dogs were different but the

same ... we would never get to the underlying issues if we would continue fighting over the symptoms ... one of our most brilliant geneticists suggested that this might be possible to randomly graft dna ... so that any couple could parent any colour ... that stage we were not a global community ... but the leader of the most colour conscious nation volunteered his family for the first cross colour birth ... it was only a small step ... but it showed commitment ... it was not just that ... some of my best friends are another colour ... the other colour was their own flesh and blood ... this was the beginning of birthtech any color can be born to any pairing of others<

Kate   You said, deeper issues, what were they?

eva   >same as any marriage my dear ... equality ... opportunity ... love and respect<

Kate   Then aGnos is really only my earth, but with the right attitude. So, like the chicken and the egg, when did it start, how, what came first? Surely you have to have peace to create more and why didn't you give the idea to the mergoplans?

eva   >you're right of course ... any system is only as good as the intensions of its sponsors ... when the G.o.d started the e.a.r.t.h the mergoplans weren't even talking to each other ... and by now ... they been suspiciously peaceful for all that time<

Kate   You are saying that peace like any other product, can be abused.

eva   >peacefulness is really only a measurement ... my dear ... the engine of peace ...

	underneath is just as important<
Kate	So, do I love my dog, because I love my dog, or because he looks after me, or both?
eva	>and as in any partnership...you respect him as you wish him to respect you<
Kate	Person to person, should I say being to being?
eva	>i would say person to person ... i'm concerned about quark ... the longer we leave him ... the more vulnerable he is ... and there's no way in the time we have before you meet the council that can show you over aGnos ... so how about i take you to the movies as you would call them ... that way least you will get a glimpse ... and we can get you home as soon as possible<
Kate	That sounds like a good idea. it must be incredibly hard for him.
eva	>you think a lot of him don't you<
Kate	I suppose I do. After all, you could hardly call swapping bodies an act of mistrust.

back in the park

Mac	They're going to the movies so Kate can look at the planet, and then she's going to address the council.
quark	*>keep a synapse in sync and let me know when<*
Ben	I think I know what's different ... you've changed your style, you're more, 'out there'. Don't get me wrong, I like it, it's ... umm ... it's in your look, your clothes and color. Have you revised your wardrobe?
Mac	Don't look at me, I'm a chauffeur not a valet, we dogs have trouble with colors remember.
quark	*>no i haven't; i dressed in a hurry and must have picked up the wrong thing ... is it very bad<*
Ben	No, no, not at all, just different, sexy ... yeah ... Anyway, here we are. it's two steps down, remember? Oh, hello ... do you have a table for two please? Good ... can we sit there in the corner overlooking the park? ... Kate, our old table is free ... have you been here since we were here last?
quark	*>have i ... Mac<*
Mac	Not unless you were sleep walking.
quark	*>no ... ben ... i haven't'*
Ben	You used to say that you could feel the trees outside, playing in the breeze.
quark	*>sounds like something i would say<*
Ben	Well, How have you been?
quark	*>busy ... the usual ... what about you ... what have you been up to ... have you made*

your millions yet<

Ben   It's funny, I think it was John Lennon who said life's what happens while you're making other plans, so after I'd asked you to marry me, and you said thanks but no thanks, I was very, I don't know, pissed off, I suppose. Then I felt stupid and inadequate and then stupid again. You know, you begin to expect something to be so and it doesn't come off, first you blame someone else, then you blame yourself. I ended up deciding that if I hadn't expected you to marry me, you would have.

quark   *>ben ... please<*

Ben   No, let me go on, Kate. I need to say this ... I'd never had to challenge myself just to do normal things, let alone the things I wanted to do. I saw that I succeeded because everything was easy, and success began to be a natural state so I had to ask myself was it love or admiration that I felt for you ... then I finally understood your incredible strength of character, and why you said no. Am I right?

quark   *>Mac ... how do i answer that<*

Mac   Why don't you just agree.

quark   *>some things i need to know Mac< ...*

quark   *>Near enough Ben ... in a way i'm an alien in your world ... i mean the sighted world ... i didn't know whether you had the experience to know if you wanted to marry me because you loved me as a woman ... or as an alien woman ... with all that implies ... as much as i loved you ... i couldn't take the risk if it meant that in a few years you* *were feeling trapped ... we didn't need that ... it wasn't easy to let you go<*

Mac   I'm impressed.

quark   *>watch it Mac ... you're paying me compliments now<*

Waiter   Are you ready to order, sir.

Ben   Oh, sorry ... yes, of course. Kate, what would you like?

quark   *>no ... Mac ... of course you can't have a plate ... you're on duty ... remember<*

Ben   Pardon?

quark   *>oh ... uh ... it's Mac ... he looks at me as if he hasn't eaten for a week ... he forgets who .... oh ... uh ... i'd like the ... um<*

Ben   How about the whiting fillets? No bones, remember? Um, Mac looks at you ...?

quark   *Oh ... you know what he ... oh ... never mind ... yes ... thank you ... whiting would be great ... do they still serve that avocado salad ...?*

memnote   *>the waiter eventually returned with the food Ben had ordered ... i could smell it ... i could not see it ... eating eggs in the privacy of the flat was one thing ... but navigating fish from the unseen plate to my mouth with only smell as a guide was entirely something else ... my admiration for Kate grew even more ... fortunately Ben seemed to have too much on hid mind to notice my un-Kate-like eating style<* end memnote

quark   *>well ... that was delicious ... thank you ... i 'm curious ... though ... how long have you*

	been coming here to see me ... why didn't you call at the flat<
Ben	I thought if I did that you might feel you had to be polite whether you wanted to or not, whereas a chance meeting in the park ... well, I was sure I wanted to see you but obviously I wasn't sure about you ... and here, if you didn't want to talk to me, you could just walk away ...
quark	*>and if i did<*
Ben	I don't know. I needed to apologize, for not being as generous with you as you had been with me. I was callow and possessive, and made separating a lot harder on both of us than it needed to be. I felt guilty about that and it didn't improve with time: some things don't. I just had to see you again and explain that, and tell you I'm sorry.
quark	*>Mac ... what happened when she sent him away<*
Mac	It wasn't easy. I had to growl at him once or twice.
quark	*>ben ... do you want me to forgive you<*
Ben	Understood would be enough.
quark	*>Mac... could you focus your very sharp brain cells on eva and Kate and tap me on the leg when Kate meets the council<*
Ben	You're very quiet Kate, how's your coffee, are you still working at the same place?
quark	*>hot ... nice ... funny about my job ... i was fired last week<*
Ben	Fired. You? Why on earth ...?
quark	*>i was attacked by a couple of thugs ... wasted lives ... you know ... kids going the wrong way ... Mac was incredible ... i wasn't hurt and they didn't get my bag but*

	... anyway ... next day ... to show due concern for my wellbeing the company decided i was a risk ... so i told old Jamesy that i quit ... anyway ... this planet never ceases to amaze me<
Ben	How many others do you know?
quark	*>oh you know what i mean ... what's the world coming to ... so i need to find myself a job quickly ... before Mac gets fat and lazy ... he dreams too much about food as it is<*
Ben	You're amazing, you are different. How do you know what Mac dreams, oh, of course, you two have an amazing ESP, I've never seen anything like it, hey, I know a guy who's looking for a receptionist, how about I ask him to call you tomorrow.
Mac	WOOF
quark	*>what's the matter ... Mac ... do you want to go for a walk<*
Mac	It's Kate. She's about to address the council.
Ben	I'm jealous about the way you two communicate. What did he say?
quark	*>oh ... he just told me that the grand council on aGnos is giving the floor to the earthling advocate<*
Ben	Wow. You and your crazy imagination.
quark	*>well what else would woof mean<*

speechtime ... aGnos

Kate   Fellow Homo sapiens: I must confess to a
period of concern at the beginning of this
trip, if I may call it that, not for my life, I
know only too well that life itself is risk.
But concern that I would be unable to
present my world in the best possible
manner.
I thought about what others might say. I
thought how a world leader would defend
his actions, justifying that sometimes
actions need to be taken no matter how
negative some of the results may be.
I wondered how an historian would
assemble his reasoning's into logical order,
giving explanations of events and their
ultimate meanings, if he could deduce them
at all, and how he may try to clarify all the
fine details on behalf of his client.
I wondered what images an artist would
send to represent and explain his world,
and whether he would be dispassionate
enough to be effective at all.
Then I remembered something my dad said
to me, when I was very young, he said,
what I did with my life was up to me, he
would love me no matter what I did. I
could wrap myself in cotton wool, or take
my chances in the world, like everyone else.
No one would ever have the right to judge
my choices but me, or maybe those who
could really understand.
I have always taken his advice as meaning,
the buck stops with me. if I don't do it for

myself no one else will, if I fail I fail because of me, no one else intervened, and I certainly fail, like all of us do from time to time. But I see that as a half full rather than an empty glass, dad said that it is better to try and fail than not try at all.

ker bajim /What do ponderous thoughts, childhood recollections and personal philosophies have to do with the current condition of the e.a.r.t.h. ... and further to that, what purpose does the council have for having this e.a.r.t.h.ling here at all, at this late hour/

Mac Who's that?

quark >the mergoplan delegate ker bajim trying to score points<

eva >as the coordinator of the council at this time i am duty bound for the sake of all concerned ... to have as much information as possible from the source ... i thought megopla would expect that ... do you have any issue with what the earthling advocate has said so far<

ker bajim /it seems to me there is nothing in her trend of speech to indicate anything one way or the other about your experiment/

eva >maybe we should let her continue<

ker bajim /as your excellency pleases/

Kate 'What I am saying, in my simplistic way, is that we don't always succeed as we would like, but, apart from that, since quark has explained the e.a.r.t.h. and its purpose to me I have wondered why it remains so important to you. I do not see that what happens on earth affects you or anyone else

and the proof of that must be that no one
has ever turned up to intervene or assist, so
why would it matter?

Now, you will have to excuse me here, if
you will, because there are so many
conspiracy theories about assassinated
world leaders, not to mention the global one
about who your own crystal really was, that
I got to asking myself why I am really here?

ker bajim /You see coordinator even your advocate
wonders why she is here/

eva >maybe if you extend her the same courtesy
that has brought the rest of us here she will
conclude here thinking and her statement<

Kate I just could not stop myself wondering. On
the one hand aGnos has built a free and
giving global culture on a high order of
planet smart technology and on the other
mergopla seems to be more fragmented like
earth, full of undercurrents, superstitions,
ambitions leaderships and conspiracies, but
none the less they are a part of this council.

ker bajim /Again I must protest, this ,this, alien
creature is using its own limited experience
to comment on something she has never
seen, never mind been/

Kate If I understand the e.a.r.t.h. correctly I am
more megoplan than aGnosic, and I think
that that entitles me to at least one
comment on the roots and purposes of the
experiment that has brought me here to
this place of justice. I have no idea how my
world would look now if the personas of
megoplans had not been sent to planet 1273
but all of my heart tells me that it would

not be the same, better or worse does not matter, it would be a product of itself. Over and over, I interrogated myself, if aGnos has been peaceful, successful and secure for eons it would gain nothing from the experiment to alleviate racial tension and hatred, but megopla would, it would gain a window, a window of opportunity, to reach inside the council, time to develop their ultimate goal, to corrupt and destroy the Council from within and turn the defensive energy of aGnos into a malevolent force to take control of everything, including the planet earth?

ker bajim /Lies, lies, outrageous lies. I do not have to be here and listen to this, blind stupid, primitive, pathetic creature accuse mergopla of conspiracy and sabotage/

Mac I told you my girl is good.

quark *>sssh Mac ... she just let 'em have it ...right between the eyes ... go girl<*

eva >no you don't. but i am equally sure that as a sign of goodwill, and dedication to pan galactic peace, mergopla will immediately, voluntarily suspend her membership and all ancillary rights in the b.I.d. as well as assist in investigations to establish and clarify the accuracy of the earthling advocate's statement<

quark *>you're right ... Mac ... she is good ... in fact ... she's as good as crystal<*

a talk in the park

Ben	Hey, Kate? What's up?
quark	*>oh ... sorry Ben ... we've been listening to the earthling advocate delivering her speech to the grand council of the b.Id. on aGnos ... haven't we Mac<*
Ben	If I'd thought whiting and avocado would have such an effect on you I'd have ... I ... does Mac want to walk?
quark	*>yes ... we should keep moving<*

memnote	*>i let Mac go back to being a dog ... while i concentrated on redeeming whatever i may have lost for Kate ... if it turned out that she cared for this male ... Ben ... however ... the seeds had been sown<* end memnote

Ben	Remember we'd sit here drinking wine out of paper cups and feed the ducks? You said you could tell one duck from another by its quack ... Kate ... I've never wanted anyone else.
quark	*>Ben ... do you believe in aliens<*
Ben	Oh Kate, not that again.
quark	*>reminiscences ... however sweet ... do not a seduction make Ben<*
Ben	What are you talking about? I'm not trying to seduce you.
quark	*>i hardly think that's Mac working on my thigh<*
Ben	I miss you Kate, terribly. I love you. I'm hoping there's something left in you for me, can we continue where we left off, no,

	before then, when I asked you to marry me?
quark	*>thighs don't talk Ben<*
Ben	Kate ... are you serious ... Okay, you win ... hmmm, let me see ... do I believe this is the only planet with people on it, maybe, maybe not. Are you still listening in on their board meetings?
quark	*>do you believe in a supreme being<*
Ben	You mean God?
quark	*>yes ... big g ... small o ... small d<*
Ben	What's that supposed to mean?
quark	*>well ... if you put a dots between letters it could mean something entirely different<*
Ben	Very funny, anyway I suppose when it comes right down to it I believe in some sort of big G little o little d God.
quark	*>does he ... she or it come from earth<*
Ben	No, he, she or it as you put it comes from a place called Heaven.
quark	*>have you ever thought that by definition ... anyone not from earth is an alien ... therefore ... you believe in at least one alien ... now if there is one there must be more ... unless he ... she or it is very lonely<*
Ben	It's not the same thing; God's the supreme one, of us. He created us in his own image. He's the ultimate earthling.
quark	*>so ... who created him ... or did he create himself ... and if he did create himself he would have had to exist before he caused himself to exist ... therefore he pre-existed his own existence and if that is the case ... who created him ... so now you have to believe in at least three aliens and if you*

follow that line of progression back through time ... depending on how long gods live there must have been a few of them and it's quite possible that the G.o.d moses knew has retired and another one has taken his place<

Ben   Kate ... what is this game? What are you on about ... this isn't all that's different about you ... are you just kidding me or, look, I'm trying to tell you ...

quark   *>yes i know ... Ben ... you still love me ... Mac are you keeping brain cells on Kate's progress<*

Mac   There's been nothing since she forced the mergoplans to back down.

quark   *>that could only mean she's on the way back ... we won't be able to communicate with her until she gets here and it also means i can't find out what to do with Ben<*

Mac   Well, don't look at me: I just love'em and leave'em; but it's great that I don't need to fret over food any longer.

quark   *>Mac ... it's all right for you ... i 'm the one entertaining the ex-Lothario<*

quark   *>Ben ... i've enjoyed this today ... it was ... er ... good having lunch here again and i would appreciate you talking to your friend about the job ... but it is time for me to go home now ... a few things waiting for me to do ... thanks again ... bye now<*

quark   *>come on Mac ...let's get out of here ... i 'm an anthropologist ... not an animal behaviorist<*

Mac   Watch it, this animal can bite.

quark   >*you know what i mean ... i have no idea if i've said and done the right thing by Kate ... has he gone*<

Mac   I've lost track of his smell at least. He's probably so confused he's gone to the pub. I hope you've still got your handbag ...

after dinner minit

quark	*>who's at the door Mac<*
Mac	How would I know?
quark	*>well ... if you sniff around the keyhole you might get some idea<*
Mac	Keyhole sniffing, what next? All right, I'm going.
quark	*>anyone you know ... we don't need a visitor at this hour<*
Mac	It's Ben. I'd recognize that pipe ten kilometers upwind in a hurricane.
quark	*>i thought we lost him at the park<*
Mac	There is a tinge of whisky on him as well. it all smells a bit if you ask me.
Ben	Kate, please, let me in. it's Ben.
quark	*>mac ... we'd better let him in ... it sounds as if he's not leaving until he says what he came to say ... but if i tell you to growl ... you break all records ... come in Ben ... i didn't think i'd be seeing you again so soon ... what's up<*
Ben	You didn't answer my question, you just left.
quark	*>which question was that<*
Ben	Whether we can be together again?
quark	*>Ben ... this is a bad time for me ... i know we meant a lot to each other once ... but you can't just walk back into someone's life saying hello ... how about we pick up where we left off ... it's a big decision and not one to make on the spur of the moment ... only time <*
Ben	Kate, we were more than lovers, we lived for each other.

quark	>*that was it Ben ... you know that ... you were living for me and neglecting yourself ... you would have woken up to that one day and ... and ...we didn't need that*<
Ben	That's why I have to see you and tell you that I have done the things I needed to do. I've made a name for myself. Your example did it for me, Kate. I owe it all to you, but there is no joy in it unless you share it with me.
Kate	I need to answer that one quark.
quark	>*how long have you been back and how come you're still disembodied*<
Kate	Long enough to enjoy the show so far. eva said that she'd leave my brainclone in place until you got back so there'll be no mistakes. Mac, how are you darling?
Mac	So far so good. I'm so happy you're back but if I start to wag my tail madly now. someone's going to get the wrong impression.
Kate	eva wants you back as soon as possible so I need to get back into my body, and you need to get going. I trust it remains in the condition in which you got into it. I take it you and Benjamin, have only been talking. You know my trip to aGnos revealed one thing about you I would have discovered no other way. In earth terms, you are quite a hunk. No wonder eva wants you back in a hurry.
quark	>*i'll ignore that one Kate ... and if you've been here as long as you say ... you know i've been fending him off for some time ... i can't see what you ever saw in him anyway*<

Kate	I should hope not, if two people who've shared each other's bodies can't tease each other what's the cosmos coming to. Okay. You'd better get going before eva starts to worry, oh, and quark, you know I'm going to miss you.
Mac	Hey, Wait a minute. Do I take it that after you've gone I will still be able to communicate with humans?
quark	>Mac ... you're sharp and practical as usual ... and you're a best friend ... i hereby appoint you earth spy first class k9 ... take care of Kate<
Ben	Kate, please ...
Kate	Ben, I am very happy you did the things you wanted to do, but don't blame me. It's only a romantic idea, doing it all for me, and maybe it got you through a tight scrape or two. I admire you for that, but don't confuse concepts with realities. Ben, I'll be your friend, your ally, even your occasional lover, but I will not be your wife. Now please go ...
Ben	Ok, Kate, I don't understand, but okay, I can't promise I won't be back, but I'll go for now, and I won't forget to ask Bob Johns to call you in the morning. See you...
Kate	What was all that about Bob Johns, Mac?
Mac	He told quark today that a friend of his is looking for a receptionist.
Kate	Oh ... oh well, all I want to think about now is sleep. it's been a funny weekend, to say the least. C'mon I think it's, bedtime for both of us...

home again

Kate	What's for brekkie today, Mac?
Mac	The beef munchies, please.
Kate	Oohhh phew ... Mac ... what's all this stuff in the sink?
Mac	Can you see it?
Kate	No. My nose is telling me.
Mac	quark wasn't the best housekeeper. He did try very hard but I was afraid that if you were away too long we'd starve.
Kate	We still might. I need to find a job, remember? Now, who's that calling at this hour, oh, yes, probably Ben's friend. Hello? Yes, good morning Mr. James.
Mr. J	Kate, I spoke with the MD. He agreed with me that the company overreacted, and he has asked me to extend to you his personal apology. I am calling to tell you that your job is here and we hope you will reclaim it, and may I add my own apology?
Kate	Mr. James, had you called at any other time, I would have said thanks but no thanks and now, I hope you understand how difficult it is for me to profusely thank the company for returning to me what it should not have taken from me in the first place. However, I do thank you for your efforts on my behalf, and, yes, we will be there today. Thanks again bye bye. What do you think of that, Mac. We're been rehired.
Mac	It'll be nice to get back to normal around here. I'm so glad you're home again. I feel like barking.

Kate	Normal, Mac, I suppose so, there are probably thousands of people out there, right now, discussing work opportunities and aliens with their doggy friends over a morning cuppa.
Mac	I take your point. Do they have dogs out there?
Kate	It's just like earth, Mac. If only we knew how to live with each other. Well, come on, we'd better get going.
Mac	Yeah, okay. I wonder what's happening on aGnos?

recipies

eva	>hello quark ... it's nice to have you back<
quark	*>do i take it our relationship has improved<*
eva	>let's just say that i'm seeing you through different eyes today ... did Kate get back all right<
quark	*>yes ... remarkable is she not<*
eva	>she certainly rattled the mergo's ... i doubt we will have any more trouble with them ... bajim had nowhere to hide and he blubbered the entire plot ... even more than we were actually wise to ... it also seems ... that now the mergoplan population knows what their leadership was planning that they are going to evict them and start again ... so now their peace looks like it will remain intact ... they have no choice really ... because they now have to reapply to be back in the b.I.d
quark	*>if they don't they'll be fair game to any of their old enemies<*
eva	>so they stay out and take their chances or come back on our terms ... the crazy thing is that they had to be superficially peaceful to make their nasty plot work anyway ... i guess it was all to do with the prize<
quark	*>aGnos<*
eva	>so it would seem<
quark	*>so the irony is ... that the experiment did work<*
eva	>but not for earth ... i would like to do something for Kate ... what do you suggest<

quark	>*why don't we leave her brainclone intact and keep a memrec channel open for her and Mac ... i've already told him that he is our new earth spy first class k9 ... he's a wonderful character ... they both are*<
eva	>brainclones are great for emergencies but they don't stay up to date with the original<
quark	>*why not just have membrain stay in touch ... he'd love that ... he could collect some more recipes*<
eva	>he could only save her from things he can communicate with ... and then only on request<
quark	>*there are enough of those aren't there ... and we can always grant him discretionary powers ... a greed*<
eva	>the least we can do<

lost and found

eva	>quark ... i'm glad you could come<
quark	*>what's wrong<*
eva	>membrain had a contact<
Mac	She's dead, quark. Our beautiful girl is dead. A bus, we were talking, I didn't see. All she said was blue. I couldn't believe that in a fraction of a moment one could feel so much, and yet so little. Before you, a pat on my back meant well done, my head in her lap meant thank you, she was my life, my god. I was a part of her world, never below love and not above reproof. But I never failed her, for that would be to fail myself, to fail my duty, to fail her trust in me. What god could ever trust a subject in the way she could trust me. What subject ever had such a relationship with their god, then you turned up and suddenly I could communicate with her. It was wonderful at first, but somehow the intimacy stemming from that made our relationship ordinary. I began to see her vulnerability, like you blundering about trying to do eggs. That perception frightened me, because in it I discovered my own weakness, yet, despite my new abilities to communicate my feelings, they defied all attempts. In fact the ability to explain seemed to stand directly in the way of explanation. So I decided that language takes more than it gives. My head in her lap meant thank you, but there were no words to explain what else it meant, And when she patted

183

me on the back for well done it meant much more any words could convey, and when I saw her swept from me, no words could convey my feelings. I hated you fro tampering with my innocence, I hated you for giving me access to another world, so making the pain or its loss more acute and unbearable, for showing me fear and emptiness, that unbearable aching that I'm sure has no peer, and no reward could justify. I failed her when she needed me most, and now it's too late to tell her that I will always love her.

quark   >*membrain ...where is he now*<

membrain   >just wandering sir ... i 'm still with him<

quark   >*let me talk direct*<

membrain   >of cause sir<

quark   >*Mac ... Mac ... you are so fortunate ...you did more than tell her ... you showed her every day ... you guided her through a lightless world*<

Mac   >I should have gone first<

quark   >*and that would have made everything better ... Mac ... Kate never gave up ... and neither must you*<

Mac   Yeah, my girl never quit.

quark   >*Mac ... you're not the only one who will miss her ... i loved her too ... you know that ... i loved her strength ... her purpose ... her courage ... but i didn't show or tell her that*<

eva   >then i did the right thing<

quark   >*eva ... what do you mean*<

eva   >a mother has certain rights<

quark   >*i don't understand*<

184

kate   >Mac ... darling ... i'm not dead ... i'm here
on aGnos ...it's up to you now ... you will
have to tell our story ... go to Ann ...Mac
...please ... go to Ann<

quark   *>this is miraculous ... are you Kate ...or
crystal<*

kate   >i am eva's ...love<
